PIZZAS *and* MERMAID
A Book of MeToo Stories

JONATHAN MONTGOMERY

Living Dreams Press
www.livingdreamspress.com

First Edition
First Printing, 2014

Cover Design by Laurie Griffin
Interior Book Design and Typography by Laurie Griffin
Cover Photo by Jonathan Montgomery

Library of Congress Cataloging-in Publication Data
Montgomery, Jonathan, 1980–
    Pizzas and mermaid : a book of metoo stories / Jonathan Montgomery
        p. cm.
ISBN: 978-0-9890941-6-0
    1. Fiction. I. Title

2014950488

Living Dreams Press
(805) 429-9252
www.livingdreamspress.com

Printed in the United States of America

To Zachary Ciperski...

Author's Note: What's a "Me Too?"

I'll pick them up late in the taxi night, when the bars are closed and the streets are empty and the moon follows us wherever we go. They'll be drunk, but quiet. I'll have to keep an eye on them in the mirror to see if they're going to puke.

"You doing alright?" I'll ask them.

"No," they'll say.

And then suddenly they'll blurt out a confession.

"I really don't like myself," they'll say.

"Huh?" I'll say.

"Yeah, I'm no good. Everyone else is doing it better."

"Doing what?"

"Life."

I'll look back at them and except for being drunk and tired they'll seem alright. I wish I could say it was just one freak with an inaccurate self-perception, except it happens over and over. A muscular bouncer. A hot college girl. An old man in a tuxedo. A mom in town for parents' weekend. A dreadlocked hippie. A starter for a college basketball team. Another cab driver. A kid in middle school. A poet I know. Men and women, young and old, rich and poor, ugly and beautiful every night getting in the cab and telling me how inferior they are.

"Now come on, man," I'll say. "I'm about to drop you off at a big expensive Boulder, Colorado house. You probably make a killing at a tech start-up and you have a hot wife and smart kids. I bet you went to a great trendy new restaurant and then drank top shelf alcohol all night. You're winning."

"No, you don't understand," they'll say. "It's taking all of my energy just to keep up. I'm in a constant state of panic and I just want to scream 'It's not alright!' but I can't because then the whole thing would fall apart. And the worst part is I'm the only one who's feeling this way."

And then I can see the problem. They don't know about all the other suffering people. They don't get to hear the cab confessions from all the diverse fellow humans like me. They only experience the relentlessly concealed truths of the sober daylight.

"You know what you need?" I'll tell them.

"What?" they'll say.

"A MeToo."

"What the hell is that?"

"It's when someone boldly admits the truth of themselves so that someone else can say "me too" and not have to feel as alone in their experience."

"And this will really help me?"

"Yes, you'll realize you're not just some freak. You'll realize people are more the same than they are different. You'll realize everything is gonna be alright. And then you'll start to actually like yourself."

"Aw, what do you know? You're just a cabbie."

"I'm not just a cabbie. I'm a poet."

"Oh yeah, Poet, well where's your book?"

"It's right here..."

Part One

PIZZAS

CONTENTS

1 / *Strategy* 5

2 / *Uniform* 6

3 / *Mixing* 8

4 / *National Anthems* 11

5 / *Real Conversations Driving Cab in Daytime:
Old Lady* 13

6 / *Pizzas and Shit* 15

7 / *The Closest Thing to the Sea* 20

8 / *Estimated Delivery Time (I)* 21

9 / *Uniting the Tribes (The Ginsberg Biography)* 23

10 / *Forcing Myself* 26

11 / *Estimated Delivery Time (II)* 28

12 / *Real Conversations Driving Cab in Daytime:
Hot Chick with Big Hungry Dog* 31

13 / *"Have a Good One"* 33

14 / *Uniting the Tribes (The New Reading Series)* 36

15 / *Tough* 40

16 / *Estimated Delivery Time (III)* 42

17 / *Real Conversations Driving Cab in Daytime:
    Out of Towner* 45

18 / *Pizza Open Mic* 47

19 / *Uniting the Tribes (Love Shovel's Mice)* 49

20 / *Driving Cab at Night You Never See Children* 51

21 / *Estimated Delivery Time (IV)* 55

22 / *She Stood Up for Me* 60

23 / *Estimated Delivery Time (V)* 62

24 / *Real Conversations Driving Cab in Daytime:
    Two College Girls* 67

25 / *Estimated Delivery Time (VI)* 69

26 / *The Last Pizza I'll Ever Deliver* 75

27 / *Uniting the Tribes (MeToo! Night)* 78

1 / STRATEGY

Sometimes pizza delivery gets really dead and no one wants to be there and each person has their own strategy to pass the time. When I was doing it as a teenager in Ohio I would take all the marinara cups and breadstick boxes and Parmesan cheese packets and make sculptures with them. It'd usually be something abstract or maybe a castle. Sometimes I'd challenge myself and make a dragon (opened pizza boxes for wings!). It would be hard to keep it from falling over, but it didn't matter cuz I think I just wanted all the other guys to see me building the sculpture and think,

"Man, this guy is a true artist and really doesn't belong here."

No one ever said that out loud. But one time this guy Craig said, "Hey, Jonny, your long hair makes you look like a chick." His strategy was to bust people's balls.

2 / UNIFORM

The National Pizza Chain's uniforms are always too big. The smallest size is like large and except for fat guys it hangs on everyone like a big baggy blob. There's always a young girl working there and you want to know the exact shape of her body but you can't tell cuz of the uniform. You have to be lucky and catch her changing before or after work.

I usta work with this girl manager who was kinda mean and would make me take a wet rag and wipe down the counters. She put in long hours and was always at the store before and after me. But one night she was leaving early and me and another driver happened to see her take her uniform top off as she was going across the parking lot to her car. She was wearing a tight white t-shirt underneath and you could finally tell she was...

...SKINNY WITH ENORMOUS BREASTS!

Me and the other guy looked at each other with wide eyes.

"Those things are monsters," he said.

"Man," I said, "you never know what's under that uniform."

Then I thought maybe there are other things we don't know about the manager. Like maybe sometimes she's actually nice and would be fun to hang out with. Maybe she knows a lot about something peculiar like the 13th century Mongol conquest of Asia. Maybe she's an artist like me and destined for a life of greatness. The thoughts kinda made me want to take off my official National Pizza Chain uniform right then and never put it back on. But I couldn't cuz I would get fired.

3 / MIXING

I didn't want to go back to pizza delivery, but I had to cuz of The Sickness. I got infected driving the taxi at night and soon I was tired and cranky all the time. I couldn't sleep and my stomach always hurt. My mind was foggy and my eyes were blurry. I had strange rashes and a chronic, snotless sneeze. I could feel a black germy goo inside me trying to spread and take over my body and when it got inside my head it made me stop laughing and caring about anything. I couldn't even write. I couldn't even watch porn with joy. It got so bad I had to go back to my parents' house in Ohio and do nothing but lay in a bed for weeks.

When I came back to Colorado I knew I didn't have the strength to go back to nighttime cabbing. I mean what was going to happen when some drunk college kid inevitably called the Fleetwood Mac I was enjoying on the radio "mom music?" I'd be too weak to fight back and get severely wounded and then The Sickness would take over for good. So I started driving daytime cab, but the money was so bad I had to do something else too. And the only thing I could get in a pinch was my old pizza delivery job.

One of the things that changed in the four years and five months since I'd last worked at National Pizza Chain was the way you prepped the pizza sauce. There used to be just a couple bags of ready-to-use sauce that you only had to empty into a bucket. But then they changed it to bags of concentrate that you had to add water to and mix. You had to use an electric mixer and it took a minute or two and it was heavy and your arms got tired after going thru a couple buckets. It would also splatter if you weren't careful and then you'd have to wipe sauce off the prep table. I'd use the mixer and think why would they have changed this to something more complicated? What's wrong with this company's decision makers?

One time I was mixing the sauce and a corporate inspector came into the store. Everyone around me stiffened up and increased their focus so they wouldn't break any rules. I didn't give a shit tho, cuz I didn't like working there again and kinda wanted to get fired. I even imagined myself getting hassled by the inspector and then getting into an argument and me saying something like, "You make too many stupid rules and I'm smarter than you."

The inspector didn't end up bothering much with the drivers tho. Instead he was extra observant of the manager and told him he was making the breadsticks too long and the extra dough was costing money. The manager had to smile and enthusiastically accept the suggestion.

"Wow, I never looked at it that way before, thanks," he had to say.

Thank god I'm not like him and barely want to be here so I can afford to be a rebel, I thought.

Later the inspector came back to where we were doing the prep and saw me mixing up that sauce and the motor was loud and the sauce was swirling around.

"Say, that mixer works pretty well, doesn't it?" he said.

It was finally my chance to complain about his corporate policies, but for some reason I couldn't remember to.

Instead I smiled and said in the loudest, most enthusiastic voice I could, "It's a lot easier than using a spoon!!!"

"I'll bet," the inspector chuckled and gave me a pat on the back.

As soon as he left I went right into the bathroom so I could look in the mirror and make a face at myself like I was choking to death.

4 / NATIONAL ANTHEMS

My Roommate was playing the national anthems again. I could hear them from the driveway when I got home from work. The front door was wide open and the anthems were coming out and I had to walk thru them to get inside The Trailer. My Roommate's back was to the door and he didn't notice me come in. He was hunched over his boombox so his ear could be as close to the music as possible.

"Hey, man," I shouted. "Let's go to The Olive Garden."

But I could not outshout the anthems. My voice was trampled underneath them and he could not hear me.

I went to my room and closed the door but they came in thru the walls. France. Great Britain. The former Soviet Union.

SYMBOLS OF STRENGTH! SONGS OF POWER! RALLYING MEN OF NATIONS FORWARD!

...screaming at me until My Roommate stopped his tape.

Then I came back out and he saw me.

"National Pizza Chain scheduled me for six days next week instead of four," he said. "And my foot is swelling up again. There are so many goddam flights of stairs in this town."

"I know," I said. "They scheduled me for two days this week instead of zero."

"FUCK!"

"Olive Garden's got all-you-can-eat pasta right now."

"Oh yeah?"

"Yeah. I'll drive."

"Okay, just give me a second."

Then My Roommate lifted himself up from the boombox, grabbed his jacket and limped his way out the door to my car. I heard him humming as I drove. The strings and trumpets and bold melodies were still playing in our heads the whole way there.

5 / REAL CONVERSATIONS DRIVING CAB IN DAYTIME: OLD LADY

DENTIST TO OLD FOLKS HOME

"I sure wish my body would get healthy again."

"Oh no, what's wrong?"

"The doctors just told me that my heart beats too fast. And who knows how long it was beating too fast before he told me."

"Man, yeah."

"Now I have to take a pill every day."

"Are you seeing any results?"

"Well, no, not at all. Except I get chest pains."

"That's not good."

"And they say when I get the chest pains I have to take three other pills and put them under my tongue and wait five minutes for each one to dissolve. And they have to dissolve separately. And you have to have a clock on you at all times so you can keep track of the five minutes."

"Right."

"And if the pills don't work then you have to go to the emergency room."

"I see."

"But the pills have worked so far."

"Good."

6 / PIZZAS AND SHIT

I always had a shitting problem...

Shit is supposed to come out of your asshole in a certain way. A reasonable amount of time after eating you start to feel a gentle fullness in your lower bowels, then you find a toilet at your leisure, sit down and after a couple of easy thrusts a long brown log worms its way out and drops into the bowl with the splashless grace of an Olympic diver. You feel light and relieved and then you're ready to proceed with your day shit-worry free.

But ever since I was a little kid it rarely worked that way for me. Most of my shits would strike out of the blue with a series of sharp, painful cramps and within minutes it would start trying to force its way out whether I was ready or not. I'd have to stop whatever I was doing to find the nearest bathroom even if I was in a middle school or a movie theatre or in a car on the highway miles from the nearest exit. I'd have to fight with all my strength to keep my asshole closed and then when I finally got to a toilet the shit would burst out violently. A hot, burning, half-solid/half-liquid explosion would bombard the bowl and the back of my thighs would get soaked in the blast.

There would be multiple attacks, waves of painful contractions, viciously loud farts and panicky asshole trembling. I'd never know if there was one more wave coming. I'd have to eventually surrender and wipe even tho I didn't feel satisfyingly finished. Often I would end up back in a bathroom several times in a row. This happened daily for years. Me thinking, I guess this is just the way I'm made, I guess I just have to put up with this. When I put the word "shit" in the title of my last volume of MeToo poems, it wasn't just to get a laugh, it really was a central concern of my life.

Then I got The Sickness and went to The Doctor and she asked me about how all the parts of my body worked.

"If your bowel movements were something from history what would they be?" she asked.

"Maybe like one of those central Asian cities where The Mongol Hordes came in and just burned everything and murdered every single person except for the artisans."

"Hmm," she said. "They're not supposed to feel like that."

"Oh," I said.

She speculated I was probably eating something my body couldn't digest. And she was right. After eliminating several common food allergens from my diet I suddenly started shitting normally. After re-introducing the foods we narrowed it down to a couple main culprits, lactose and gluten. Which is basically anything that's made from milk or wheat. Did I have Celiac Disease, the medical condition in which your body's immune system attacks a piece of bread as if it's the flu virus? Or have they genetically modified the wheat plant so much that almost all of the human species now have some degree of intolerance to it? Or is it something else? I don't know. I just know not eating these things make life better for me.

Before when I used to work at National Pizza Chain the store's products were the foundation of my diet. The breadsticks, the cinnamon sticks, the cheese bread, the cheese dots, the Parmesan bites, the pasta bowl, the subs, the brownies, the cookie pie, and of course every variation of pizza. When I returned I realized there was nothing on the menu I could comfortably eat. All of it was bread and cheese and sauce.

One day I came into work and the prep table was covered in bread and cheese and sauce. Pieces of it. Splatters of it. Busted sculptures of it. There was one mad scientist in the middle of it all. He was wearing a jumpsuit with the NPC logo on it, and he had an evil grin on his face.

"Who's that?" I asked The Shift Leader.

"That's The Owner's Asshole Son," he said. "He manages the whole business for him now. Don't do anything wrong when he's here. He likes to fire."

I just wanted to stay away from him. I was tired and didn't feel like trying to say the right things to somebody. I'd worn stained pants that day and my hair was long as always. But I had to do the prep somewhere.

I cleared a small space on the edge and got out a box of chicken wings and a box of tin foil. I ripped out several squares and then wrapped up ten wings per sheet and then threw them into a plastic bin. The Owner's Asshole Son looked over at me.

"Hey!" he said. "You ever hear of National Pizza Chain's New Product Contest?"

I didn't answer.

"Well," he said. "Anyone who works for the company can enter a new recipe. Corporate judges them all and if they pick yours then your product gets on the menu at every store in the nation. I'm trying to win this year."

He pointed at his mess.

"Check it out," he said. "It's The Pizza Inside a Pizza."

Then he started making a new one and walking me thru the steps.

"First you make a regular medium pizza with whatever you want on it. Then you put it between two extra large crusts. And then you put more sauce and cheese and toppings on top!"

It sounded a little crazy but I'd seen similar new products before that must've won the contest. Endless configurations of bread and cheese and sauce. All doing the exact same thing inside your body, but people thinking it's something brand new and buying it. What would happen if you entered sushi or hummus in the New Product Contest? What about an apple?

"Here," The Owner's Asshole Son held up a slice of The Pizza inside a Pizza, "This one just came out of the oven. Try it."

I looked at it and could clearly imagine myself getting intestine-fucked on a delivery later that day. It'd be an emergency and I'd have to ask the person at the door if they would let me in so I could use their bathroom. They'd reluctantly agree and then I'd be in there for a long time. And their toilet would have some special trick for flushing that I wouldn't know and my poop water would be unable to drain and it would rise up to the top of the bowl. It would be so visible when the person had to come in and do another special trick I don't know about to make it vanish. This might not even happen just once that day. It might happen two or three more times.

"No thanks," I told The Owner's Asshole Son.

"Oh, c'mon," he said. "It's gonna be fuckin' good."

"I'm alright, man."

"Don't tell me you're on a diet. You're too skinny."

"No, I'm not on a diet. I just can't."

"What do you mean? You don't eat meat or something? You want a veggie one?"

"No, that's not it either."

"Then what then?"

It seemed like to properly explain I'd have to go thru everything—the lifelong nature of my shits, the biology of wheat, The Sickness, why I was there at all. It seemed like it would take too much energy so I just shook my head and said nothing.

The Owner's Asshole Son kept looking at me tho, squinting in confusion. I tried to ignore him and focus on the chicken wings. But then suddenly he lunged at me and stuck a slice of the new product right in front of my mouth.

"Feed your face!" he said. "Or I'll fire you!"

All his muscles were flexed and his eyes looked like cheese and bread and Mongolian death. It made me freeze up, not knowing if I should knock it out of his hand or surrender and take a bite.

Before I could make a move tho, he started laughing and pulled away.

"Just kidding, haha," he said. "I wouldn't fire you . . . for that."

Then he gave my ponytail a little tug. And then I pretended like there was a delivery up.

7 / THE CLOSEST THING TO THE SEA

The 28th Street McDonald's parking lot was pretty big and the Applebee's next door had just closed so there were lots of empty spaces. You didn't have to pay for them and no one from McDonald's was going to come out and hassle you for not being a customer. There were many seagulls and it smelled like Filet O' Fish sandwiches. It was the closest thing to the sea in Boulder, Colorado.

I would dock my taxi-ship there under the shade of the trees, roll down the window, let the air come in my nose and go, "Ahh." At lunchtime other workers would come and throw down their anchors next to me and we'd nod at each other thru our windows. All the sail-vans and pickup-boats with ladders on the roof and company phone numbers on the side doors. The hardworking Mariners of Boulder taking deep breaths as they sprinkled extra salt on their French fries. The birds going, "Tweeg, tweeg, tweegull." And we'd all think what a nice little harbor to escape to during the mid-day storm of job.

My parents used to take us to a beach on Nantucket Island every summer but it was never as sea as that parking lot.

Word had it a Trader Joe's would soon open up where the old Applebee's was and then the busy shopping people would need all those spaces. It would once again become middle-America landlocked pavement and we'd have nowhere to dock but the sea of our own imaginations.

8 / ESTIMATED DELIVERY TIME (I)

National Pizza Chain had a new computer system that kept track of how long it took you to make your deliveries. The computer also kept track of how long it *should* take you. You'd come back from a delivery and clock in and the computer would say something like "actual delivery time: 18 minutes," and also say something like "estimated delivery time: 12 minutes."

I knew my identity went beyond just delivery guy and didn't want to care about things like being good at it. But I couldn't resist looking at the numbers anyway. And I noticed I could never seem to beat the Estimated Delivery Time.

"What the hell?" I'd say. "I've been driving professionally in this town for nine years. It's not possible to take better routes than I'm taking."

I went up to the guy known as Our Fastest Guy and asked him about it.

"Hey," I said, "do you know how they calculate this Estimated Delivery Time?"

"I don't know," he said, "Why?"

"It seems a little out of reach, doesn't it? Once I got a minute off but that was the closest."

"I don't know what you're talking about. I beat it all the time."

"All the time?"

"Yeah, a good driver should be able to."

After that I started driving a little faster and swearing more when I'd wait at a red light. But I still couldn't get under the Estimated Delivery Time. I was feeling bad about it and wondered if maybe I was somehow just unnaturally slow. Then I asked My Roommate who also worked there and was known as Our Oldest Guy.

"Oh yeah, it's bullshit," he said. "You can't beat it. The system is fixed."

"But Our Fastest Guy says he beats it all the time," I said.

"He's lying. I've seen the computer after his deliveries. It thinks he's too slow too."

"Well, how do they come up with the times?"

"I don't know. The higher ups probably fuck with it. The faster we go the more money we make them."

"But they're making us feel more stress."

"They don't care about that."

"I don't like it. Maybe we should do something about this."

"Look, I've been doing this a long time. I've learned it's best to ignore this kinda thing. Just go at your own pace. If they don't like it, fuck 'em. They ain't gonna fire you."

"Yeah, I guess you're right," I said and knew I'd have to remind myself more frequently how superior I was to the job.

9 / THE GINSBERG BIOGRAPHY (UNITING THE TRIBES)

I was over at My Poet Friend's place, sunken down in the bottom of his chair and saying things like, "No one cares about my poetry anymore. I've been sick too long and the Boulder Poetry Scene isn't the same. Maybe I'll never go to a reading again."

"I know what you need," My Poet Friend said and grabbed a book off his shelf, "The Ginsberg Biography."

Allen Ginsberg—famous 20th century American poet, center of the Beat literary movement that rose to national prominence in the 1950's, countercultural icon, student of The Dharma, co-founder of the Jack Kerouac School of Disembodied Poetics at Naropa University, where I once got a Master's of Fine Arts in Creative Writing. I knew the biography.

"Get that outta my face!" I said, "All thinking about Ginsberg does is make you sad you don't live in an era when poets didn't have to deliver pizza cuz pizza delivery didn't exist yet."

"You're only remembering The Myth of Ginsberg," he said. "If you read this book you'll be reminded that Ginsberg was a real human person who got down about himself and his times just like you. But then he grew to become this…"

Then My Poet Friend pointed to a photograph standing on his desk. It was of a hairy-bearded, Indian-clothed 1960s Ginsberg captured in mid-dance with a look on his face of pure euphoria.

"Let me see that," I said and got up and took a closer look.

There was just something about it. Some kind of hope for life was trying to leap out of it and into my body whether I liked it or not.

"Well, there is a lot of reading time driving cab in the day," I said.

"Yes," My Poet Friend said. "You'll need to read something. Take this with you."

I ended up taking it with me every day to work. I'd go park in the 28th Street McDonald's parking lot and read uninterrupted for the 30, 46, 63 minutes between fares during the slow dayshift. I was able to get fully inside the world and reality of Ginsberg. My favorite part was when he was working for a market research company and told his psychiatrist he hated jobs and only wanted to be a poet. The psychiatrist said something like, "Why don't you, then?" and then Ginsberg actually did. The rest of his life all he had to do was travel around the world and read poetry and party. It MeToo'd me well and I started getting ideas.

"What we need is a big reading," I told My Poet Friend. "Like the Six Gallery reading, San Francisco 1955, when Ginsberg first read "Howl." He brought the East Coast and West Coast beats together and from that day forth they were a force to be reckoned with in the culture."

"Yes!" My Poet Friend said, "Poets are the most important thing that can happen for a culture. We speak the truth and have the courage to be ourselves and influence others to be honest and courageous too."

"The Boulder Poetry Scene is divided right now. Every man and woman for themselves, feeling alone in their struggle to make an impact. But if we come together it could be like Genghis Khan and how he united all the Mongol tribes until they were a Horde strong enough to take over the world's largest continent. This could be us. Uniting the Boulder Poetry Tribes. Genghisberg!"

"We are not about bloodthirst, tho."

"No, we're about MeToo. And the big reading will be called "MeToo! Night." And everyone will celebrate the unified Boulder Poetry Tribe by reading their most honest autobiographical poems. We'll all feel so great about ourselves and have the confidence to launch forth and reclaim our rightful, glorious place in this culture!"

"Yes! It must be done."

"Let's start at once."

10 / FORCING MYSELF

A lot of times in the middle of the afternoon there was nothing to do. It was between lunch and dinner and there were no pizzas to deliver. We'd already prepped the chicken wings and the drainables and cut the sandwich bread. We'd mixed the sauce and poured the cheese into the plastic bins. We'd labeled the expiration dates on everything. We'd restocked the fridge with Coca-Cola products, taken out the trash, wiped down the counters, broken down cardboard boxes and thrown them in the recycling. We'd swept and mopped the floors and started the dishes. We'd folded enough boxes so that every stack went to the ceiling. We'd even scrubbed the inside of the oven hood. There was nothing left to do, but National Pizza Chain has a policy that employees must be doing *something* at all times while on the clock and the managers were enforcing it. We should've been celebrating. We'd finally caught up. But if you just stood around, the manager or even someone more powerful might see you and say something devastating like, "Don't stand around."

One thing I did to look busy was go to the bathroom. First I'd make it look like I was scanning the room for another task vital to the store's success. Then I'd go, "Ah," and stride with purpose straight to the toilet. I'd close the door behind me and lock it and then I was safe.

While inside I'd try to stretch out every step of a normal bathroom routine. I'd take my time unbuckling my belt, pulling the zipper down on the fly of my khaki uniform pants, and pointing my penis over the bowl. Then I'd stand there waiting for something to come out.

"C'mon," I'd say to my penis, "I need to have a reason to be in here."

But nothing would happen. Maybe I'd just peed not too long ago. Maybe I hadn't had anything to drink. Sometimes at work I felt so dry inside.

"Dammit," I'd say.

Then I'd remember that forcing it never helps. I'd take a deep breath and relax and after a few moments I could feel a little liquid starting to move thru me. Three or four trickles of urine would finally fall out and drop into the toilet and I'd be so proud of myself.

Then I'd flush and wash my hands for the full twenty second requirement as posted over the sink. I'd dry my hands with paper towels until there was absolutely no more water on them and then I'd look up at the mirror. I'd watch myself take another deep breath. I'd say "Alright, time to go back out there," and hope something had come up that needed to be done.

11 / ESTIMATED DELIVERY TIME (II)

For a while I was able to ignore the Estimated Delivery Time and go my own pace just like My Roommate said. It was nice. Sometimes after a delivery I'd stop at home and take a piss and make a turkey sandwich on a gluten-free bun. Maybe I'd make it with cucumbers and shredded carrots and honey mustard sauce and it would be very delicious. I was still making alright money and figured I could take the job for a while longer if it was like this. But then one day I came to work and there was a memo on the wall over the computer.

> *No one here is going fast enough! Our customers need their pizzas right away or else they'll never order from us again. But we are consistently slower than the Estimated Delivery Times. Everyone needs to stop being lazy and go faster. The computer knows which of you are good workers and which of you aren't. Here's the list...*
>
> *— Mgmt*

Then there was the list of all the drivers and what their average delivery time was for the week and what their average Estimated Delivery Time was. My name was only a couple from the bottom.

"This is bullshit," I said. "I'm a day driver. There's more traffic when I'm working, but the EDT doesn't seem to account for it. This statistic doesn't accurately reflect anything."

The Shift Leader shrugged at me.

"Maybe you can clock me in before I get back from deliveries," I said. "Just to even the playing field."

"But if I get caught doing that I might get in trouble," he said. "The Asshole Manager hates me I think."

"Fine. I don't even care. So what if everyone thinks I'm the worst worker?"

But for some reason I couldn't help but care. I looked at the list all the time. I started to see its stats even when I wasn't in the store. I'd be out on a delivery and see a very red "#19 of 21" at each traffic light. Suddenly there would be "Our Fastest Guy + 1:01, Me + 5:39" running out across the road. How could I miss them? The numbers were right on my steering wheel. Right on my windshield. I even started to see them on my pillow when I went to sleep at night.

I tried to take things up a notch and started speeding through every step of a delivery. I'd rush out of the store even if it meant forgetting two liters and Parmesan cheese packets. I'd run out to the car and then drive over the speed limit all the time. I would beep my horn extremely loudly at all the other cars on the road.

One time I was coming up to an intersection and didn't see any other cars so I just drove straight thru the stop sign.

"Yes!" I said and pumped my fist. "Five more seconds off the delivery time!"

But then a cop car came up behind me and made me pull over.

"I have to go this fast for my job," I told the officer.

But she didn't care and gave me a ticket for BAD DRIVING and I had to pay $100 to the city of Boulder even tho that was more than I'd make that day.

"Man," I said to The Shift Leader when I got back, "if you woulda just clocked me in."

"It's not my fault," he said. "I didn't come up with the list. The Asshole Manager did."

"Well, then maybe I'll confront him about it."

"Okay, but he's been in a really bad mood lately."

"Yeah, I've noticed that too."

"He might get really mad at you. He might yell. Or blame it on you somehow."

"You think?"

"Yeah, and remember, he's more powerful. He can fire you but you can't fire him."

"That's true."

"If I were you I'd just pay the ticket and lay low."

"Yeah, maybe you're right."

Then I grabbed the next order and ran.

12 / REAL CONVERSATIONS DRIVING CAB IN DAYTIME: HOT CHICK WITH BIG HUNGRY DOG

APARTMENT TO SUSHI ZANMAI VIA TABLE MESA KING SOOPERS

(HER ON PHONE WITH SOMEBODY)

"The King Soopers pharmacy is going to have a lawsuit on their hands."

"I was supposed to pick up my prescription at the 30th Street one that's closest to me, but instead it was all the way down at the Table Mesa one. And I had to take a cab there and now I don't have enough time to get a book before I go to jail for the next eight days."

"I need you to pick me up a book."

"Because I have to go to Sushi Zanmai to get one last decent meal."

"A book on yoga."

"Something with a lot of poses in it."

"I don't know, like thirty bucks. Just spot me and I'll get you back."

"One with a lot of poses, like with lots of pictures of the poses."

"Not hardback cuz you can't have hardback in jail, only paperback."

"Yeah, one with just like a ton of fucking poses, and also the first two volumes of *50 Shades of Gray*."

"Overnight the shit and send it to me in jail. I'll pay you back. I'll go crazy if I don't have a book or something."

(HER TO ME)

"Sorry you had to hear that."

"No problem."

(SHE GOES INTO KING SOOPERS, BIG HUNGRY DOG COMES UP TO FRONT SEAT AND BITES SANDWICH I WAS SAVING FOR LATER)

13 / "HAVE A GOOD ONE"

My Poet Friend was complaining about one of his co-workers and how she'd always say, "Have a good one!" to the customers at their coffeeshop.

"Have a good one?" My Poet Friend said. "Have a good what? She repeats it and doesn't even know what it means. It's like she's a tape recorder."

"I see what you're saying," I said. "That is not a very poetry way of living."

"Yes! We have to live like humans instead of machines."

The truth was I said, "Have a good one," all the time at my jobs, but after that conversation I decided not to anymore.

In fact, the next time I delivered a pizza I didn't use any worn-out pleasantries at all.

"Hi, how are you?!" the woman who answered the door said.

"You owe me 19 dollars and 38 cents," I said.

"It's a nice day out isn't it?"

"19 dollars and 38 cents."

The woman frowned and when she paid she only gave me a 62 cent tip.

I called up My Poet Friend and told him what had happened.

"The problem was," he said, "you didn't say anything."

"What should I say, then?"

"Something that relates with The Reality of the Moment."

"Alright."

Then I went on my next delivery.

"Hey, what's up, man?" the guy at the door said.

"I hate pizza delivery," I said. "Look at what I'm forced to wear. It's so bright blue and red. I look like a clown. My car is making bad noises and I've had to pee for like the last three deliveries but haven't for some reason. I think I've internalized the critical voice of my boss. Why am I doing this? I have a Master's degree."

The guy looked at me strangely as we completed the transaction.

"I wonder how many people have lactose and gluten intolerances like me but don't even know it," I said. "I wonder if you're one of them. This cheesy pizza will fuck with your digestive system all day 'til you violently shit it out. I don't really have any hopes or wishes for you about this. I will forget about you as soon as I'm back in my car."

The guy didn't say anything and then shut the door. My tip was $0.00.

I called up My Poet Friend again.

"Enough of this," I said, "I'm using the pleasantries again. They're essential to work success. I don't care if I sound like a tape recorder."

"I guess if you think you have to," he said. "But maybe at least try not to use 'Have a good one.'"

On the next delivery a sweet older couple answered the door.

"Oh, wonderful, our pizza is here!" they said.

"Yes!" I said, "I hustled down here so you could get it fresh and hot … How are you folks doing today?"

"We're doing very well, thank you. How are you?"

"I'm doing great!"

"That's great to hear."

"Now all I need is for you to put your signature on this credit card receipt and we'll be all set. Here, use my pen."

"Alright, thank you."

Then they filled out the receipt and wrote in a five dollar tip.

"Thank you very much," I said. "I really appreciate it!"

"No," they said. "Thank *you!*"

I was acing it and all I had to do was say a friendly goodbye. But the time was about quarter til five and my mind couldn't commit to either "good night" or "good afternoon" and when I spoke a hybrid of the two accidentally came out…

"Have a good nightfernoon!" I said.

The sweet older couple looked at each other and laughed.

"I mean, have a good *night*," I had to say.

"Haha, you too, dear," they said and then I left.

The whole way back to the store I was embarrassed and kept swearing and repeating the words "good nightfernoon" to myself. I saw then just how useful "have a good one" really is and decided I'd have to use it all the time again. Except of course in front of My Poet Friend, but he was never around my work anyway.

14 / UNITING THE TRIBES (THE NEW MONTHLY READING SERIES)

In order to unite the tribes I had to start going to the readings again. Each tribe had their own. There was the Oldest Reading in Town, The Full Moon Reading, the Anarchists' Reading, The Poetry Bookstore's Reading, and The Denver Readings. The Mountain Poets read at Love Shovel Ranch. And the Grad Student Tribe read at The New Monthly Reading Series.

It was started by a Grad Student fresh on the scene. We hadn't met and she didn't know about me, but it didn't take long to hear about her. She apparently had tremendous organizational skills and wasn't afraid to ask local businesses to use their space for a poetry event even tho they probably thought poetry was weird. She would also fearlessly post the events on Facebook and hang up professionally-designed posters and do interviews on public radio shows.

"Who the hell does she think she is?" I said to My Poet Friend. "She's acting like a reading series never existed in this town before her."

"But you can't unite the tribes without her," he said. "You'll have to go to one."

"I guess you're right," I said.

I easily found the time and location for the next New Monthly Reading

Series reading and went by myself. It was in the back room of a new hip Boulder restaurant. You had to pay a five dollar cover to get in, even tho poets don't have any money. But when I got there the large room was packed. Every table was full of people. There was a stage and lights and it looked like everyone was there for Rock n Roll.

"Genghis Christ!" I said to myself and took a seat near the back.

I remembered that I didn't really like crowds or meeting new people. I just wanted to hide in the shadows and judge everyone.

"Oh no," I thought, "What if I don't have enough Ginsberg in me to unite anything?"

I mean I just couldn't help getting annoyed. Grad Student was hosting and she'd get up on stage and do things like *welcome us* and *announce the readers*. She'd adjust the microphone for whatever height the reader was. She got an email list going around so you could sign up and learn about future events. She led a round of applause to thank the space for having us.

"Disgraceful," I thought. "She's trying to take over the world without me."

Then there were all the Grad Students who read. Their work was very experimental and too brilliant for me to understand. I just couldn't MeToo any of it. I was signed up to read, but I wondered if my stuff was too *un*experimental for them to MeToo. I felt like leaving early. I felt like giving back The Ginsberg Biography even tho I hadn't even got to his death yet.

"And the next reader is something called Jonathan Montgomery," Grad Student suddenly said.

I was taken off guard and didn't know what else to do but go up to the stage. All I had to read were a couple of things I'd just written about pizza delivery. I looked out into the crowd and they looked back at me. I figured they'd probably never had stupid jobs before but I had to read my stuff to them anyway.

The poems were all about how boring and bothersome the National Pizza Chain was and I was soon strangely energized by reading them. I received the strength to hold my body up straight and make clear resonant sounds from my mouth. And the energy built and then I was stomping my feet and shouting the words. Lines about managers and uniforms and sauce came firing out of me. At a crucial moment in the piece I even grabbed a nearby chair and got on top of it and screamed at my loudest with my fist in the air.

"Take that, boss!" I read. "Take that, survival and economic reality! You make me do things I don't want to do!"

When I was finished I leapt off the chair and took a bow and the audience actually applauded. And later Grad Student and some of her tribe approached me.

"Great reading," one said. "I think pizza is hilarious and poignant and delicious all at once."

"Me too," I said.

"I used to work at National Burger Chain," another one said.

And we knew to hug each other right then.

"We're going to the bar now," Grad Student said. "You're invited to come with us."

And then I went with them and got to see her and her tribe up close and realized I was all wrong about them.

"My plan for the New Reading Series," she said, "is to go beyond just the Grad Students. I want to meet and feature all kinds of people from the Boulder Poetry Scene. Maybe even the Colorado Poetry Scene. Maybe even the National Poetry Scene."

"Yes!" I said and told her about uniting the tribes and MeToo! Night.

"It seems then that we are on the same page," she said, "and I will bring my tribe to your event."

15 / TOUGH

I remember this one time working at National Pizza Chain when I was seven years old. They had me on the cut table. I had to take the pizzas out of the oven, and then slice them and then put them in a box. I was small and had to stand on top of a stool to get the job done. And the pizza peel was very heavy for me and my arm would shake as I scooped the pies out. And the blade was very sharp and I didn't want it near my fragile skin. And I didn't have the strength or the right aggressive stroke to cut all the way thru the pie. But they had me keep doing it anyway.

The deep dish pizza was the hardest to do. You had to hold the pan in one hand with a metal tong, cut around the perimeter with the other hand and then flip it from the pan into the box. One time a deep dish pizza came out and my wrist accidentally touched the side. It was white hot and it made me go, "Ouch!" and I dropped the pan. I had to stop everything so I could hold my wrist. Nobody noticed until pizzas started falling. The conveyor belt would slowly push the pizza to the edge of the oven and then it would fall face down on the floor and cheese and sauce would splatter.

"Hey, kid, what the fuck?" the manager said.

"I burned myself," I said.

"So what? Get back to work."

"But it really hurts."

"You gotta toughen up, Montgomery."

And then I started to cry. Loudly and red-faced with lots of tears.

All the manager said was, "Move!"

I moved over and he started cutting the pizzas himself. I couldn't stop crying. All the guys were looking at me. I was useless. They had to call my parents to pick me up.

When Mom and Dad got there I told them what happened. I said I had to quit but they wouldn't let me.

"That's just how the world is," they said. "Everyone has to work."

And the next day after first grade I had to go back to NPC and pull things out of the oven again.

"You're not allowed to cry here, no matter what happens," I said to myself.

And for the last 25 years I haven't.

16 / ESTIMATED DELIVERY TIME (III)

I actually lived with The Asshole Manager. He had a room at The Trailer too. He was on the other side next to the bathroom and we both stayed in our rooms a lot and the only time I saw him was when we accidentally had to use the bathroom at the same time.

He hadn't been The Asshole Manager at first. He was once just The Pizza Maker and needed a cheap place to live like the rest of us. When he got promoted I figured he was making a lot more money but for some reason he didn't move to a better place. The Trailer had its way of keeping you trapped there.

At work I could see why people were calling him The Asshole Manager. Everything he said to people was about something they were doing wrong.

"Not enough pepperonis on this."

"I don't care if you have class that day. Job's more important."

"Answer the fucking phones, bitches."

It made you never want to talk to him at work.

One night at The Trailer we both had to use the bathroom at the same time. At the same moment I was going in to pee, he'd just finished peeing.

"Uh," he said.

"Uh," I said.

Then as we were shuffling thru the door he stopped.

"I hear you got a ticket," he said.

I shrugged.

"That's no good," he said. "If people see you pulled over with the top sign on, it makes NPC look bad."

"Well, since you brought it up, it was only cuz I was trying to go faster to make NPC more money."

"No one told you to go thru stops."

"It's the stupid Estimated Delivery Time list, man. It's making all the drivers stress out trying to beat each other. And soon some guy is going to go so fast he'll wreck his car and die."

"That's not my problem."

"But it was your idea to put up the list. You're the one who decided we needed to sacrifice everything for a pizza store."

"It wasn't my idea. It was The Owner's Asshole Son. He made the list. He said if we got closer to Estimated Delivery Time he'd give me a big bonus."

"Greedy!"

"You don't understand. I make no money. I need it."

"Bullshit, managers have lots of money."

"No, they only pay me in bonuses if the store makes a certain amount of money. But we never make it. I made more as a pizza maker. Why do you think I still live in Trailer?"

"I didn't know."

"I didn't even want to be the manager. They made me just cuz I'd been there the longest. I hate it. Everyone thinks I'm an asshole, but The Owner's Asshole Son is the real asshole. He's always yelling and saying he's going to fire me. If you don't like Estimated Delivery Time, you tell him."

"But he's never going to listen to me. I don't even know how I'd get to talk to him."

"Not my problem."

"Rrm," I said and then went in to pee.

17 / REAL CONVERSATIONS DRIVING CAB IN DAYTIME: OUT OF TOWNERS

GAS STATION TO TABLE MESA KING SOOPER'S VIA WALGREENS VIA FOOTHILLS HOSPITAL

(HER WHILE HE WAS INSIDE WALGREENS)

"Can you put on the AC?"

"It's on, but I can put it on full blast I guess."

"It's really hot."

"I know."

"Colorado's a dry heat at least. Not like Atlanta. Atlanta's real hot."

"Is that where you're from?"

"Yeah...say, do people actually go on that mountain over there?"

"Yeah."

"What do they do on it?"

"Like hike and bike and rockclimb."

"Why would they want to go up there?"

"To be in nature, I guess."

"Have you ever been on it?"

"Yeah."

"Aren't you scared you're going to fall off?"

"No, most of it's flat enough that you can easily stand on two feet."

"It looks scary."

"It's not."

18 / PIZZA OPEN MIC

Every week there's an open mic at National Pizza Chain and everyone who works there gets to sign up to read their latest poetry.

At the last one a guy read about all the girls he was probably going to have sex with.

"I'm glad my wife got me arrested on that bullshit domestic violence charge," he read. "Now we're getting divorced and I can finally have sex with anyone I want."

The audience clicked their fingers.

"This one chick has been texting me nonstop," he read.

Then he held up his phone so we could see a picture of her and she was very average looking.

Another guy read a piece about gross and kinky terminology you can learn about on urbandictionary.com.

"The Dirty Sanchez, The Rusty Trombone," he read.

I'd heard that poem before at other NPC open mics. And something very similar at my middle school lunch table open mic. But it seemed to be fresh to this audience's ears and they were inspired to participate. They shouted out their own lines like "Cleveland Steamer" and "Donkey Punch."

"Blumpkin," the reader concluded and everyone erupted in laughter.

Another guy was a real performance poet. He read about mixed martial arts and illustrated with quick kick-and-punch combinations.

"I can take anyone here," he read.

"I could take you," a heckler said.

"No, you can't."

"Prove it."

"I would if we weren't at work," he said and got off the stage.

The last guy read a political poem about U.S. President Barack Obama.

"If elected to his second term," the guy read, "he will unleash his secret Socialist armies and all the real Americans will be thrown in jail."

The audience was shocked.

"Don't have any credit cards," he read, "cuz that's how they find you."

When the open mic was over we all clapped and went back to work.

"Hey, Jonny," one of the guys said, "How come you never sign up for the open mic?"

"I save all my stuff for another open mic," I said.

"There are other open mics?"

"Yeah, lots of them. One's at a poetry-only bookstore."

"What do they read about there?"

"Like flowers and the moon and reality. You should come next week."

He said he might, but he never did. I guess he was satisfied with the open mic he already went to.

19 / UNITING THE TRIBES (LOVE SHOVEL'S MICE)

I went up to the mountains to Love Shovel Ranch to talk to Marcus and his tribe about the state of the Boulder Poetry Scene. I brought a bottle of Jameson and they fed me a meaty stew and we agreed there was a lot of energy in the air and it was time for the tribes to unite.

Then they brought out a mouse. It was trapped in a small plastic cage.

"The house's got a mouse problem," Marcus said.

Then they opened the lid to the cage and stuck in the spout of a water bottle. But instead of water it was full of red wine.

"They ain't like yer pet store mice," Marcus said. "These mice're cannibals."

I looked at the mouse thru the yellow plastic cage and its fur seemed prickly and greasy.

"When we put them in a cage together, one always ends up getting killed," Marcus said, "They'll find the weak one, murder him, and then eat him."

The mouse was ignoring the bottle of wine.

"Knows it's poison now," Marcus said.

Then they brought out another one.

"Just got this one from the live trap," one of his tribe said.

It was in a clear jar with holes poked in the lid. One of his tribe had a marijuana pipe and he took a hit from it, exhaled into the jar and covered the lid with a book. Then all the animal could breathe was marijuana smoke and he started trying to jump up out of the jar.

"Thinks he's asphyxiating," Marcus said.

But soon the mouse calmed down and then he curled up at the bottom. I looked at his eyes and they were black and staring straight out.

"Is he stoned now?" I asked.

"Let's see," Marcus said.

Then he picked up the jar and started slowly rotating it. The mouse lost his balance and fell on his back and his feet were in the air and he was helpless to correct himself.

"He's stoned," Marcus said.

Everyone laughed and then they opened his ventilation back up and soon the mouse began to move around normally again.

"I'm having a big poetry reading," I said and told them about MeToo! Night. "You and your tribe should come."

"Ay," Marcus said, "We'll be there."

20 / DRIVING A CAB AT NIGHT YOU NEVER SEE CHILDREN

They're never passengers and you don't pass them on the streets, because they're asleep in a bed at home. When I was only working nights I would see absolutely no children for weeks at a time. I'd forget they existed. I could see how this could be a world of only drunk adults in which *I* wasn't even a child once. I just started life sometime in my late-20s and I didn't have parents.

Then when I started working days I saw them again. They'd be walking across a crosswalk in front of a school or they'd be inside a bus pointing at me from the back window and I'd be like, "Oh yeah, kids."

One weekend day I got a bell at the movie theatre and when I got there like ten kids charged at the car. They opened the door and started coming inside. "Oh, god," I thought. "They think I'm a toy." I desperately looked around for the *real* fare and hoped they could help me shoo them out. But when an adult finally appeared he told me I had to take five of the kids to a certain address while he followed with the other kids in his car.

I looked back at them in my mirror. Children. Up close. It was like looking at the rearview mirror at the zoo. I drove extra cautiously and under the speed limit so I didn't accidentally damage any of the kids. It was nerve-racking and I wanted the ride over with.

"It's my birthday!" one said.

"Okay," I said.

"Guess how old I am?"

"I dunno, twenty-one?"

"No. I'm nine."

"Oh," I said.

I didn't know what else to say to someone that age.

"Can we play Cash Cab?" the kid said.

"Yeah!" all the rest of the kids said.

"What do you mean?" I said. "You want me to ask you questions?"

"Yeah!"

I tried to remember what I knew when I was nine. That was the year I won the school's Geography Bee.

"What country has the most population?" I asked.

"China," one said.

"Wow, that's actually right," I said.

"Yay!" they all said. "What do we win?"

"Um . . . twenty five cents off the fare?"

"Yay! Give us another question."

"Alright then, for another quarter, how many electoral votes does Colorado have?"

"Nine," one said.

"Wow, you know things. That's a total of fifty cents off."

"Yay!"

"Who was elected president in 1980, the year I was born?"

"Umm, Bill Clinton?"

"No."

"George W. Bush?"

"No."

"We don't know then."

"It was Ronald Reagan."

"Never heard of him."

"Well, he was a real president once. He won the most electoral votes ever in 1984."

"Hey, do you know what movie we saw?"

"What?"

"*Wreck it Ralph.*"

"That arcade movie?"

"Yeah."

"Was it good?"

"Yeah."

"Are you gonna see that Abraham Lincoln movie that's coming out?"

"No, that's too scary."

"No, you're thinking of *Abraham Lincoln, Vampire Hunter.* This is just the regular Abraham Lincoln movie. It stars Daniel Day-Lewis."

"Did you see the movie *This is It*?"

"The Michael Jackson movie?"

"Yeah."

"You know who Michael Jackson is?"

"Yeah. He's awesome."

"Alright, we're almost there. We have time for one more Cash Cab question."

"Yay!"

"For another whole dollar off the fare, name three Michael Jackson songs."

"Thriller," one kid said.

"Billie Jean," another kid said.

"Beat It," another kid said.

"Yay!" I said. "You got it!"

"Yay!" they all said.

Then we got to the address and I showed them how the meter said $9.00 but I was only going to charge them $7.50.

"Yay!" they said again and then all got out of the car.

Then the adult who was following us got there and came to the window.

"How much do I owe you?" he said.

"Seven," I said.

21 / ESTIMATED DELIVERY TIME (IV)

The next time I came into work there was a new memo.

Still going way too slow, guys. Customers are calling in to complain DAILY. This has got to stop. It's time to "trim the fat." The slowest driver on next week's list will be fired.

— Mgmt.

Then there was a new list and at the very bottom it said…

Jonny Montgomery

It's not that I would've minded getting fired, but I was behind on a couple things and my credit cards were all maxed out. I needed some time to catch up before I could just leave NPC and drive daytime cab full time. Also I didn't want to be known as the guy who got fired for being too slow.

"Haha, you're going to get fired," a driver saw the list and said.

"It was that damn football game last Saturday," I said. "I was the only one working and you couldn't get near campus without getting stuck in traffic."

"Didn't you used to be a cabdriver in this town? Didn't you used to work here for like years before that? Seems like you should be faster."

"Can't you see the problem isn't me? It's the list."

"I like the list. It lets me know who sucks and who doesn't."

"Yeah, but if I go and you take over my day shifts then you'll suck."

"Won't happen to me. I'm number three."

"Rrrg."

Just then The Owner's Asshole Son came in. He grabbed some sauce and cheese and dough and headed straight back to the prep table. We'd already finished all the prep and were just standing around.

"Find something to do!" The Shift Leader urged us.

The other driver grabbed the broom and starting sweeping a dirtless floor.

"Damn, I shoulda thought of that," I said to myself.

My only option left was to go to the bathroom. But I had to go past The Owner's Asshole Son to get there. He stopped me before I could make it.

"Hey," he said. "Come over here."

Then I had to come over there.

"I'm just going to the bathroom," I said. "Then I'm going find something to do."

"This'll just take a moment," he said.

Then he pointed at the ingredients in front of him.

Look!" he said. "I'm making The Reverse Pizza. Crust on top, cheese in the middle, sauce on the bottom."

"Okay," I said.

"You can try it when I'm done."

"Thanks, but I'm good."

"Oh, come on. This is going to be awesome."

"I told you before, I can't eat this."

"What do you mean *can't*?"

"I can't. I'm…"

"You're what?"

"I'm on a gluten- and dairy-free diet."

"Oh, god!"

"What?"

"Gluten-free?! Gluten-free's not real. It's just something health snobs came up with to feel superior to other people. Eating a pizza crust isn't going to kill you."

He was looking at me like *I'd* done something wrong and suddenly something came over me. All the frustration and rage from working the bullshit job came bursting out. It made me lunge at him and stick my finger in his face.

"Now look here," I said. "You don't know what you're talking about. If I eat this I am going to get violent diarrhea. Burning, smelling, watery shit that feels like knives going thru my intestines. And not just once, but several times for the next day or two. I'm not going to put up with that just so I seem normal to you."

"Who do you think you are, sticking that finger in my face?"

"I'm Jonathan Montgomery."

"Montgomery? Aren't you Our Slowest Guy?"

"No. I'm Our Smartest Guy. I have a graduate degree. And I'm one of the premier poets in this town. My powers of insight and observation are exceptional. And I can see all the bullshit of this entire operation. Especially the Estimated Delivery Time."

"What do *you* know about business?"

"In the two-and-a-half months since I've worked here again, half of the drivers have quit. Everyone's too overstressed. We're understaffed, our times are worse than ever, you're not making money and it's not because of us, it's your own policies."

"Come with me right now."

The he grabbed my shoulder and led me into the office and closed the door behind us.

"Fire me if you want," I said. "I don't care."

"No," he said. "I'm not going to do that."

"Why not?"

"Because you're right. The EDT *is* bullshit."

"Ah ha!"

"It wasn't my idea. It was My Asshole Dad's. He said we needed to increase our bottom line at all costs and this was the way."

"When I last worked here four years and five months ago there was no list and business was fine."

"You're probably right. Since the EDT, we're actually making less money."

"How can you put up with this, then?"

"You don't understand. I can't say no to My Asshole Dad. He's a self-made man, but I grew up with everything handed to me. When he gave me control of the NPC franchise it was my chance to prove myself. I've never been good enough for him. I thought making him a ton of profits might make him finally respect me."

"You don't have to do this. Talk to him. Tell him EDT doesn't work."

"No, no, I can't. I've accepted the situation. I'm just gonna have to bust my ass for my dad's approval the rest of my life. Maybe I'll win the New Product Contest and that will help... Besides he would never listen to me anyway."

"Maybe he'll listen to me."

"You? But you're just a driver."

"I'm not just a driver. I'm a poet."

"But he doesn't care about poetry."

"He won't be able to help it. Poetry is the most powerful thing there is."

22 / SHE STOOD UP FOR ME

I went out for a walk. I had to go thru the whole trailer park to get to the bike path and then I went for a couple miles just free-associating pairs of words and trying to see what I could accidentally make strange and poetic...

moon dick

tiger barista

pizza goo goo

I'd look at a tree or a prairie dog or a cyclist and think...

apple guitar

midnight morocco

or

detective sneeze

Then I didn't feel like walking anymore and I went back thru the trailer park home. I looked at each trailer I passed and free-associated words with them...

astronomy trailer

napoleon bonaparte trailer

hooters trailer

Then someone yelled out, "Hippie!"

I looked ahead and noticed there was a bunch of kids playing football in the middle of the street. As I got closer one of them said it again, "Hippie!" and another one said, "Hobo!"

I thought about what I looked like and remembered I had long hair again and was wearing a red bandana to keep it out of my face. I was also wearing sunglasses and a jean jacket and jeans. It seemed normal to me but I guess I looked like something to them.

"Hippie, hobo, hippie, hobo," they kept saying.

Then one of them said, "Hey, stop it."

It was a girl. I'd seen her in the neighborhood before. She was probably around 12 and was on the verge of being pretty. Sometimes when I walked by she'd stare at me and I'd wonder if she had a crush on me.

"Stop what?" one of the boys said.

"Calling him names," she said.

"So what?" he said.

"So you wouldn't like someone calling you names. It's unpleasant."

Nobody called me "hippie" or "hobo" again after that. I wondered if it was because they had a crush on her. I liked how she used the word "unpleasant."

unpleasant trailer

pleasant trailer

pheasant trailer

Batman trailer

trailer Rock n Roll!

23 / ESTIMATED DELIVERY TIME (V)

I got The Owner's Asshole Son to tell me where his dad's business offices were and on my next day off I barged in. I went up to The Asshole Owner's secretary and demanded she schedule me for an appointment.

"No way," she said.

"But it's urgent," I said. "It's about one man making everyone else's life slightly more miserable in exchange for his own personal gain and we all hate that."

"I hate that too, but I'm in total fear of The Asshole Owner. I have children and depend on his paychecks. What would happen if I messed up and got fired? My children would starve? No, my mothering instincts won't allow it."

"Fine, I'll just wait here til he comes out."

"No, you're going to get him in a bad mood and then he'll take it out on me. He yells. He yells so much."

I didn't want to cause any harm to the secretary so I left. I wondered if I'd reached the limits of my access to the powerful.

"Dammit," I said to The Shift Leader next time at work. "I was so close to bringing down the Estimated Delivery Time. I guess the system is just rigged against us."

"Yeah," he said. "I guess that means you'll just have to deliver this next one as fast as possible."

Then he handed me two pizzas and the price said $0.00. Also the label had a note on it that said "DON'T FUCK UP."

"What's this mean?" I asked The Shift Leader.

"I don't know," he said. "Didn't take the order."

"Man, I hate these free ones. You know it's cuz we're making up for something we fucked up already and now they're going to stiff *me* for it."

The Shift Leader didn't care tho, and I had to take the delivery.

It was in the neighborhood of huge old fancy mansions. Sometimes those houses are the worst tippers even tho they could give you $100 and they wouldn't miss it. When I got to the door an old guy in a suit came out. It seemed like the pizza delivery tip had probably been invented after his time. But I still had to try and not fuck up anyway.

"Hello, sir," I said. "How are you today? I have a piping hot and fresh pizza for you and it looks like it's free of charge."

I handed him the box and he took it.

"I like your manner, son," he said. "I also like how you sprinted out of your car. You seem to be a real hustler."

"Thank you, sir."

"Tell me, what makes you work so hard?"

"They're just my values, sir."

"Terrific."

Then he handed me a ten dollar bill. The biggest tip of the whole month.

"You've impressed the right guy," he said. "You know I'm your boss, right?"

"What?"

"I am. I'm the Owner of the Boulder National Pizza Chain franchise."

I looked at him closely. I tried to see if his face was rotting a little more cuz of his position in life. The lines in it were thick. The skin was gray. It was disgusting.

"Ah ha, fate!" I said and handed the tenner back to him.

"I don't understand?" he said.

"I don't want your dirty money, Asshole Owner. I don't like you and your greedy policies and the reason I hustled to the door is not cuz of my values but because you and your bullshit Estimated Delivery Time forced me to at gunpoint!"

Then I pushed my way inside and confronted him with the whole story, whether he liked it or not.

"Have you ever looked at it that way before?" I said when I was finished. "Your decisions affect other people's stress!"

I expected him to yell and kick me out, but he didn't.

"I'm not heartless," he said. "I started out as a delivery guy myself and I feel for you. But what do you want me to do about this?"

"You're the one in control of this thing. Change the EDT back to realistic numbers or just destroy it forever."

"I'm afraid I can't do that."

"Why not?"

"I wasn't the one who created it."

"Then who did?"

"Corporate."

"Who's that?"

"They're the ones who make up all the rules. They're the ones who come up with the uniforms and the products and employee code of conduct. They're the ones who design the computer software."

"What would happen if you broke the rules?"

"They could close the store and fire me and all the management and employees."

"Maybe they wouldn't find out?"

"Haven't you seen their inspectors? They're here all the time. They come randomly and without warning. They know everything we do."

"Well, we need to get thru to them somehow then. We need them to realize the EDT is bad for The Earth."

"Good luck with that. *I* can't even get a private meeting with Corporate."

"But you're a millionaire."

"But they're billionaires."

"We can't just give up, tho."

"We can. They're just too powerful for us to win. Besides if it wasn't for them and their name brand, neither of us would have any money. I suppose we could start our own Independent Pizza Store but regular people are so discomforted by new things. We could even have a better product but the only ones who'd try it would be rebellious-minded freaks and there wouldn't be enough of them to make any money. We'd get crushed."

"I don't believe you. I've been told I couldn't get thru to any of the levels of management above me in this company but I have every time. I know there's someone at the top of this pyramid and I'm going to reason with them and they're going to change."

"You've got a lotta fire, son. And the tongue of a poet. And I actually may know of a way we can do this. But there's too much risk for me. You'll have to do it on your own."

"I'm discovering that's the only way I'll be able to do this. I'm ready."

24 / REAL CONVERSATIONS DRIVING CAB IN DAYTIME: TWO COLLEGE GIRLS

APARTMENT TO CAR PARKED ON HILL CUZ TOO DRUNK TO DRIVE IT HOME NIGHT BEFORE

(TO EACH OTHER)

"Joe is so hot."

"Joe is hot, but he's kinda mean."

"I know but mean is kinduv hot."

"True."

"The first time I saw Joe I was like, 'oh my god, abs.'"

"Josh is like that too."

"I think Josh wants you."

"I think so too."

"I can't believe we let Jason come in with us last night."

"I know."

"Guys make the strangest noises when they cum."

"Haha, yeah."

(TO ME)

"I'm sorry you have to overhear this, haha."

"It's alright. I used to drive nights and every fare talked like that."

"What do they talk like in the day?"

"It's all like children and old ladies and they don't talk about who they have crushes on."

"Aww, do you miss the drunk kids?"

"I do, but I also like the children and the old ladies too. I feel like I'm starting to like everyone now. I'm feeling healthy and strong."

25 / ESTIMATED DELIVERY TIME (VI)

I came into the store a couple hours early like The Asshole Owner told me. When I got inside I saw them. One guy was at the cut table wearing an insider's uniform and an apron. He was holding up a deep dish pizza pan with a pair of tongs. A woman with a clipboard was nearby telling him to do things. To the side was a cameraman operating a big Hollywood-style movie camera. Behind them were a row of men in suits, including The Asshole Owner. He winked at me.

"Alright, action," the woman said.

The cut-table guy held up the pan in front of the camera.

"National Pizza Chain's new deep dish pizza!" he said.

"Again," the woman said.

"National Pizza Chain's new deep dish pizza!"

"Again."

"National Pizza Chain's new deep dish pizza!"

"Again."

"National Pizza Chain's new deep dish pizza!"

It went on like that for about fifty more times saying the words slightly differently each time.

"Okay," one of the suits finally said, "let's take a break."

Then they all gathered round and started talking to each other except for one of the suit guys who started heading toward the bathroom. I rushed back and cornered him before he could get in.

"Oh, I'm sorry," he said. "Do you need to use the restroom too? You can have it first."

"No," I said, "I don't need the bathroom. I need answers."

"Alright, how can I help?"

"Why did you make that guy say 'deep dish pizza' so many times?"

"We're trying to get the commercial perfect."

"And why do the commercial here?"

"Cuz it's the closest store to the advertising agency. Boulder, Colorado is our hippest and freshest market."

"Are you with the agency?"

"No, I'm with National Pizza Chain."

"How powerful are you?"

"I'm the CEO."

"The very top?"

"Yes. That's enough questions. Now let me pee."

"Not quite yet. I need to know one more thing. Are you the guy who came up with Estimated Delivery Time?"

"The EDT?... What do you care about that?"

"I'm a driver here and it's ruined my life."

Then I told him the whole story.

"Hmm," he said. "I was afraid of this. I never liked the EDT. It always seemed to me people are already going *too* fast in this modern age. I actually suggested a rule that all NPC drivers go at a pace most comfortable to them. I mean who wants a sweaty, panicky, stress-crazed guy coming to your door with your food? It's just unpleasant."

"But you're at the very top. Who could overrule you?"

The CEO gave a deep, long sigh.

"The Man in the Closet," he said.

"Who is he?"

"It's hard to explain. He doesn't work for the company, but I must take orders from him."

"Take me to him."

"He's a real asshole. If you say the wrong thing to him he could destroy you."

"I'm not afraid of assholes anymore."

"What, you have some kind of super-courage? Who are you?"

"I'm The Poet."

"My whole career I've been dominated by The Man in the Closet. I've prayed nightly that one day someone would come along and stand up to him for all of us. Someone supernaturally strong in their convictions. A Chosen One. Perhaps that one is you and the day has come."

"It is and it has. Let's go."

Then the CEO peed and then took me on his private jet and flew us back east to the Corporate Headquarters. The place was like a castle with colorful flags and great walls and guards everywhere. We were transported to the top by helicopter, then descended in the elevator 'til we got to a whole floor that was the CEO's office. It had ping pong tables and golden statues, pet crocodiles and an all-you-can-eat buffet. It had its own orchestra and the smell of freshly-baked bread was pumped in thru the vents. Framed on the wall was an original bow and arrow once used by a Mongolian warrior in the sacking of some helpless Asian city. You could still see a dead defender's blood on the arrow's point.

"This was all made possible by The Man in the Closet," the CEO said.

"Take me to him," I said.

Then he led me into a smaller and simpler private room. It only had a waste basket and a desk that was empty except for a placard that said "CEO." There were no windows. On one wall was a closet door.

"He's in there," the CEO said and pointed to the closet.

I went ahead and opened the door carefully. A light inside was slowly revealed.

"Oh my god!" the CEO said.

I expected to see some kind of government agent or one of the Aliens or probably just The Beast, but instead it was completely empty. A few square feet lit up with bare shelves. Not even office supplies or a coat.

"There's nothing in here," I said.

"Yes, there is," he pointed. "The Man in the Closet is right here before us."

"Is he invisible?"

"No, he's just standing there. Can't you see? Can't you hear him telling us to get a pizza?"

"No."

The CEO put his ear closer to the closet.

"What's that?" he asked the empty space, "We have to get it to him in the next 30 seconds or else?!"

I looked into the CEO's eyes and they were a cloudy black and seemed to be looking into the other dimension.

"You're a crazy person!" I said. "You're taking orders from nothing."

"Oh no!" he said, "Only fifteen seconds left!"

"Nothing's going to happen!"

"Yes it will. The Worst will happen. Do something, Chosen One!"

The CEO crouched down and trembled like the greatest bomb ever was going to blow us up. But at the end of thirty seconds nothing happened.

"Nothing happened," I told him, "can we get rid of the EDT now?"

But the CEO didn't answer. He was still crouched down and trembling. And I realized I would never be able to change any of the National Pizza Chain's policies.

Maybe every company has a Man in the Closet or maybe it was just this one, but either way I knew what I had to do.

"I quit," I told the crouched man and gave him my two-week notice.

"New deep dish. New deep dish. New deep dish," he said.

I could only shake my head.

"Have a good one," I told him and left the office to find the helicopter and fly away.

26 / THE LAST PIZZA I'LL EVER DELIVER

The last pizza I'll ever deliver was to a poet. His name is Tootles and he'd started a thing where every full moon people gather at midnight in an alley behind Pearl Street to read their poetry. We knew each other and it was a coincidence that out of all the drivers and customers that night I got him and he got me.

It made me think of the first pizza I ever delivered and how it wasn't to a poet. It was to a mom in suburban Akron, Ohio. I pulled into her driveway and rang her doorbell and she came out and I handed her the pizza and she paid for it plus a tip.

"Hey," I thought, "what an easy way to make money."

And then I ended up taking like thousands more deliveries off and on for the next thirteen years.

When I made that first delivery I didn't know any poets or even think about knowing any. I wanted to be President of the United States of America and know people who could be my Vice President. I was about to go Washington, D.C. for college and it was all very possible.

But after a few hundred more deliveries I started to change. I realized my favorite thing to do was observe things and put it into words and that I was probably, by fate, supposed to be a poet. And then I started making decisions like I've got to go to a college that's good for writing. And I've got to move around and get experience. And I've got to avoid a career cuz that might distract me from my true passion. And these decisions led to thousands more deliveries. There was no time to learn any other job and it was easy to get hired in any town I went to and when no one was paying me for what I really loved to do. Whenever the job sucked for me I just had to say, "This is just what you have to do to be a poet" and then I felt like it was honorable. And I was able to do it for a long time before I finally couldn't any more.

Thousands and thousands and thousands of deliveries. So many deliveries it would be boring for me to even guess. Delivering to people I didn't know. No one knowing me or why I was doing it. How many thought I was still just an 18-year-old doing this temporarily with a bright future of capitalist potential? How many thought I was just some unskilled member of the society? How many would've laughed if they did know what I was?

I got into cab driving eventually and liked it for similar reasons and it was a lot better. At least you didn't have someone tell you when you had to work or when you could go home. At least you didn't have to wear that stupid bright blue uniform. At least when it got tough it still seemed cool in a dark, gritty Robert DeNiro kinda way.

When I came back I was too much of a poet by then to handle more than a few final deliveries. The last pizza I delivered was to another poet and we hugged when I came to the door.

"This is my last delivery ever," I told him, "and I'll write about this and read it at the next full moon."

"Cool," he said.

Then I invited him to MeToo! Night and he said he'd come and then we hugged again.

When I got back to the store it was slow enough to let me go home, but The Shift Leader asked me to take one more.

"No," I said.

"Are you sure?" he said, "It's a close one."

"No, that had to be the last one," I said. "It was to a poet."

"What does that mean?"

"It's just something that's important to me."

Then he shrugged and let me go.

27 / UNITING THE TRIBES (METOO! NIGHT)

It was a Saturday night and there we all were at the Poetry Bookstore. I'd moved all the seats and tables and brought the stage and microphone into the larger center area. People sat on the benches and seats around the edge of the wall and there was a big open space in the middle, which I'd filled with balloons of every color. I'd also brought all my costumes for people to wear. And all my stuffed animals for people to play with. When they came thru the door I handed them neon signs that said "ME TOO!"

I'd summoned all the poets of The Boulder Poetry Scene I knew. Ones who were my best friends and allies. Ones who I'd just met. Ones who never made it to readings anymore. Ones who'd locked themselves up in their house after the divorce. Homeless ones. Ones who'd been kicked out of readings before. Ones who had to let go of their grudges. Ones who'd mysteriously vanished. Ones who were currently out of state. Ones who had to find a babysitter. Ones who were children. Ones who'd randomly been in the cab. Ones who'd received a vision in their dreams to come. Ones who were not poets at all but just worked at a national pizza chain. Ones who I delivered pizza to for my last delivery ever. The ones from Love Shovel. And the ones from the Grad School Tribe. All the ones came together as one.

And everyone got up to the mic and read autobiographical things about their reality. Something they wanted everyone else to know about them, even at the risk that people couldn't relate, out of the hope that maybe they would and then they'd both feel less alone. And I told them whenever they thought "me too" they had to hold up their bright sign and scream the words out loud so everyone knew.

And every few readers I'd yell out "DANCE BREAK!" and loud music would come over the speaker like Little Richard and Hall & Oates and Chumbawumba and everyone would fill in the open floor and move their bodies wildly and toss up balloons and everyone would bat at them to keep them in the air and when Florence + The Machine's "You've Got The Love" came on I got up on a bench and waved the MeToo Flag that I'd made out of a stick, a garbage bag, and spray paint and I watched over as everyone on the dancefloor was hugging and laughing and singing along with looks on their faces of pure euphoria.

We were united and we were ready to take over the entire world...

Part Two

MERMAID

CONTENTS

1 / *Mermaid* 84

2 / *Restaurant People (Moth)* 86

3 / *The Goddess of Faith, My Guardian Angel Who Loves Me No Matter What* 89

4 / *After Sleeping with Me* 91

5 / *Placenta* 94

6 / *David Byrne Had Very White Hair* 97

7 / *Unicorn* 99

8 / *Smelled* 103

9 / *Weekend at Fairy's* 106

10 / *My Fingernails are Scattered all over the Streets of Boulder, Colorado* 113

11 / *Carelli's Fire* 115

12 / *The Giant* 117

13 / *Mohawk* 121

14 / *The Fortune Teller*   123

15 / *I Liked the Boulder Flood!*   128

16 / *The Sorceress*   132

17 / *The Beauty of Autumn*   134

18 / *Wand*   136

19 / *Things that Get Left in the Back of My Cab*   138

20 / *The Sorceress's Kiss*   143

21 / *The Gas Station Guy Watches Me Play the Lottery*   146

22 / *Sex with The Sorceress*   150

23 / *The Lexus Bow*   153

24 / *Voucher Bookmarks*   156

25 / *My Eyes*   159

26 / *It's Alright*   164

27 / *Angel and Mermaid*   168

1 / MERMAID

The last time I went home I went to The Aquarium with my mom, dad, brother, sister-in-law, five-year-old nephew and three-year-old nephew. The nephews started running as soon as we got inside, even tho you needed to stand still to watch or read everything. Sometimes they would stop to push a button that would make a noise or start a video or make something spin, but then they'd just start running again a second later. I don't know where they were running to and why they had to get there quickly. Maybe it was The Greatness at The End of The Aquarium. But whatever it was the whole family had to run with them, cuz if the children ran alone they could go past The End of The Aquarium to Beyond The Aquarium and there they could get lost.

I was running with them for awhile, but then we got to the mermaid part and I had to stop. I had to read the information about them like how they help rescue shipwrecked sailors but they're getting overfished and now they're an endangered species. There was a video there about someone who once found one on a beach in Australia, but the mermaid was dead and seagulls were pecking it for meat. The Aquarium also had a mermaid skeleton hanging upright by wires and it was like a human skeleton except it had bones for one long fishtail instead of bones for two legs. And they also had a glass cage full of water and there was a living mermaid inside that. It was a girl mermaid and her seashell bikini was lying on the bottom and you could see her boobs and they were pointy and you could see her pubic hair poking thru her fins and it was bright turquoise like the hair on her head and the hair on her armpits. I stood in front of the cage and watched her but she didn't look back at me. Then I pushed the button to make her sing and it appeared as if she was trying to but the soundwaves couldn't make it thru the water and the glass for you to hear anything. I pushed the button again but the same thing happened and maybe it was broken.

Then I looked around and noticed my family wasn't near me anymore. I had to leave the mermaid part to find them and I realized they'd probably gotten far away and then I had to run thru The Aquarium faster than I thought children could go. I ran thru every part, but I still didn't find them.

Then I wondered if they were looking for me and I thought staying in one place would help them do that. So I went back to my favorite part of The Aquarium—mermaid. When I got back someone had made her put her seashell bikini back on and she was swimming in circles and some kids were pushing her button but couldn't hear anything.

I watched her for a while and then my legs hurt from standing and I had to sit down on the floor. And then my neck hurt from holding up my head and I had to hold my head with my hands. Then I just looked down at my shoes. I was hungry and Mom had said earlier that she'd packed snacks for everyone. My stomach growled. I yawned. I kept waiting…

2 / RESTAURANT PEOPLE (MOTH)

Every night from 5pm to 9pm the Restaurant People come to downtown Boulder to go to restaurants. I see them driving their cars trying to get to the restaurants and there are not enough parking spots for them and they cut each other off and honk and stalk people who seem to be getting in their cars to go home, and then they wait for them too long and block up the road and you can't get around them.

Wow, I think, something really awesome must be going on in those restaurants. I don't know what it is because I don't go to them. I only have $300 a month to spend on food and the supermarket is the only way to do that and have enough calories to live.

Last week I was trying to park out front of the poetry open mic and there were no open spots. I noticed the restaurant next door was completely full of Restaurant People. More people than I'd ever seen at any poetry reading ever. It was just a weekday night, but there they were and they'd needed every single nearby parking space.

I wanted to know once and for all who the Restaurant People were and why they were there and what kind of jobs they had and what kind of houses they lived in and what kind of poetry they wrote and how often they were afraid about absolutely nothing at all for no reason. I wanted to know why they had to be in a restaurant every single night of the whole week.

I had to park my car several blocks away and then walk back to the restaurant. I looked into the window but not too closely in case they'd see me and ask me to go away. There I saw the Restaurant People eating meals. They would take a fork and dip it down to their plate and then spear a piece of food and put it in their mouth. Sometimes between chewing food they would speak to each other and I don't know what they were saying but they would laugh sometimes. It all seemed very normal and it seemed like I should be in there with them. That is until the moth came in…

It was flying outside and got attracted to the restaurant's glow and flew inside. It landed on a lamp and it didn't seem like it wanted to do anything but stay on the light, but the Restaurant People saw and made the Restaurant Workers get the moth. "UGLY!" someone said and then they put the moth on a table in the middle and all the Restaurant People stopped eating and got up and stood around it. Then they started performing surgery on it. They used little surgical instruments to remove the moth's body parts. Legs. Tail. Wings. Face. Fur. Brownness. All taken off and separated on the table and then set on fire with a match. Little flames burning the parts of the old moth quickly and disappearing. Then all the Restaurant People held hands and sang "The Moth Killing Song":

Dead moth, Dead moth, Dead moth

When they were done they went back to their tables and started eating with their forks and mouths again as if nothing odd had just happened.

I'd seen enough and ran over to the open mic and signed up to read. When it was my turn I got up to the microphone and said, "Alright, we all need to sing 'The Moth Alive Song.'"

"What's 'The Moth Alive Song'?" the audience asked.

"I don't know, but we have to right now."

"Alright," they said.

And then we tried to sing it.

3 / THE GODDESS OF FAITH, MY GUARDIAN ANGEL WHO LOVES ME NO MATTER WHAT

Every spare moment I was working on the novel, a longform of literature necessary to master if you ever want to become a commercial success. The main character was me and the love interest was The Goddess of Faith, My Guardian Angel Who Loves Me No Matter What. Whenever I doubted myself she would rub my shoulders and fill me with a magical substance called It's Alright, Baby and then I would feel alright. The novel was autobiographical and I swear The Goddess of Faith was a totally real part of my life once.

For one whole era of my life I would summon her every night before I went to sleep.

"Goddess of Faith, can you please be in my dreams tonight and help me in case they turn into nightmares."

"Of course, baby," she would say.

And then I'd have a dream about a haunted house and a ghost would jump out of the closet at me and go "boo!" But then The Goddess would throw her body in front of me like a shield.

"Stand down!" she'd say to the ghost.

And then she'd start talking to them and we'd realize they were just scared too and needed someone to listen to them.

But the Goddess would also be around when I was awake. She would come with me to school and work and parties, giving me hugs of It's Alright, Baby when I most needed it. My best friends were all familiar with her. I mean I and anyone else who wanted to could totally touch the fabric of her angel tunic and the softness of her goddess skin. It wasn't a big deal.

But at some point I forgot how to summon her. I couldn't remember if it was thru some great sacrifice or just saying the right magic words. I couldn't remember if maybe I didn't even need to summon her, cuz she'd just come on her own, but she wasn't anymore cuz I did something wrong and now she hated me. The closest I could get was writing a novel about her and it wasn't the same. I'd yell at it all the time.

"C'mon, manuscript Angel!" I'd yell. "Be real."

But she wouldn't be anything more real than words.

It made the novel really hard to write. It made me hate the novel but I felt like I had to keep writing it so the world would love me and then pay me.

4 / AFTER SLEEPING WITH ME

One thing you do after sleeping with me is look at the painting over my bed. It's abstract with lots of swirls and streaks and splatters of different colors and boldnesses. And when you look at it for a while you start to see faces and animals in it. There's a wizard. There's a half-wolf/half-dolphin. There's a pair of tits, several of them.

Me and the person I sleep with play a game to find new things hidden in the painting. Knights and minotaurs and penises. They like sleeping with me and they like the game and then we sleep together again. And then I think yay, they like the painting, they like the game, they like sleeping with me, they like it, they like me.

But then there's always the time we play the painting game for the last time.

"I see the dragon," the person I sleep with says, "and everything around it is dying under its flames even tho it doesn't want to die."

"I don't see it," I say.

"What about that mopey coward?"

"Where?"

"There. His face is serious and his back is hunched and he does nothing to fight the dragon."

"Maybe we should look in another corner of the picture."

"There then, in that corner is The Beast."

"The Beast?"

"Yeah, and there's you next to him."

"No."

"Yes. You're there with your small stature and smooth cheeks and your microphone and red glasses. And The Beast is hovering above you and controlling everything you do."

"No. There's no Beast in there."

"Yes, there is. Look at his hairy belly. Look at his fists and scowl. Beast."

"No. You're misinterpreting. There are only Angels in this painting."

"I know a Beast when I see one."

"Angels."

"A Big Bad Beast."

"No!"

"Yes! Yes! Yes!"

"Get out of my bed!!!"

Then they don't sleep over anymore after that conversation.

And then when I'm all alone again The Beast comes.

"You fucked up, Jonathan," he says. "You let them see me."

"I know," I say.

"Don't let them see me again."

"I know."

"Hide me better."

"I will."

"No, you won't."

"What if someone who sleeps with me sees you and doesn't mind?"

"Impossible."

"I know."

"Hide me better."

"I will."

"You're not a good hider. And you won't."

"I know."

5 / PLACENTA

"I want to be happier," the woman in the cab said.

"Well," the man in the cab said, "I heard someone say if you give one second, just one second, of every hour to someone else and their needs, that will make you happier."

"But I do give. I give every single second of every single hour to the kids."

"I know."

"I just…I just want to have an orange and like really feel its roundness in my hand and really taste its sweetness in my mouth. I just want the full experience of life. You know?"

"I know."

Their conversation made me think of my grocery list and how I wanted to get oranges that week. And also a placenta.

When I went to Whole Foods the next day they had oranges but I couldn't find the placenta.

"Did you find everything you were looking for?" the checkout girl said.

"No," I said. "I want a placenta, but it doesn't seem like you have it."

"Oh, I think I've heard of that. That's like some kind of new superfood, right?"

"I don't know. I just want it, tho."

Then she scanned and bagged my groceries and I paid for them. And then she told me to go to the customer service desk to ask about the placenta.

"Placenta?" the customer service guy said. "I don't think I know what that is."

"It's a thing that feeds a baby inside a uterus."

"And you want to eat it?"

"No, I want to eat from it."

"I don't understand."

"I want to connect it to my belly button and have it send nutrients straight into me."

"Do you know who manufactures it?"

"It's not artificial. It's real and made of flesh."

"From a mother?"

"From my mother."

"But your mother only had a placenta for you just that once."

"If something existed once it can exist again."

"Like by magic?"

"No, by reality."

"Alright, I'll look into it. What's your mother's name?"

"Her name is Every Single Second of Every Single Hour."

The customer service guy wrote it down.

"Alright," he said. "I'll see if I can get that in stock for you."

"Thank you very much," I said.

Then I left Whole Foods and tried to eat one of the oranges in the car on the way back home. Its juice dripped down my wrist and it was too wet and sticky and I wished I had a napkin.

6 / DAVID BYRNE HAD VERY WHITE HAIR

I just saw a Youtube clip of David Byrne performing with St. Vincent on Letterman and David Byrne's hair was very white...

Just like it was back in the 1970s when he was beginning his music career with The Talking Heads. Byrne was very old even back then and he was respected for his white hair and his cane to keep balance on stage and the punks at CBGBs lovingly called him Grandpa.

And he had the song "Psycho Killer" which is a song about being crazy and wanting to kill people. It became a hit because everyone knew it was created from decades of life experience and they were in awe of David Byrne's wisdom. They knew only such an elderly man could get over his ego enough to just make up nonsense sounds like Fa-fa-fa-fa-fa-fa-fa-fa-fa-fa. And they respected the slightly off-key tremble in his voice that suggested he was way too old to be concerned about immature things like sex and money anymore.

David Byrne had such white hair that kids fresh on the New Wave scene would dye their hair white too and pretend they were triple or quadruple their ages. But they could only write songs about falling in love in high school and they were quickly exposed as frauds. Their songs didn't become hits and at concerts people would yell at them,

"Grow up" or "Come back when you're in your sixties, then maybe I'll care."

David Byrne had white hair and Debbie Harry wasn't blonde anymore and the Ramones were totally bald.

And each song the Talking Heads came up with was better than the last, like "Once in a Lifetime" was better than "Psycho Killer" and "Burning Down the House" was better than "Once in a Lifetime." Cuz they wrote each song with a little more life experience than the last one. They only stopped coming up with new songs cuz they eventually had enough experience to understand it was no longer spiritually wise to be in a band anymore.

Then David Byrne went solo and his new songs didn't sound a lot like the Talking Heads and people were like, "Wow, he's so aged he's bored with everything he used to be doing," and they wished they'd been alive long enough to be that bored.

And now David Byrne, beyond medical explanation, is still somehow alive and is collaborating with the young St. Vincent and giving her the credibility she would have no way of achieving at such a young age in the music world. And they get up on stage and play rock music with various obscure brass marching band instruments and it's very advanced. And Byrne is an intense combination of stiffness and flailing and Byrne's hair is very very white and his eyebrows are also white and he has lines on his forehead and a loose Adam's apple and it makes me feel very good. My hair is still light brown and I'm not supposed to be great at art for another several decades. There's so much time left and I can just relax.

I just want to relax.

7 / UNICORN

Me and the poet Get in the Car, Helen went to the strip club once and there was a Unicorn there. She looked like a regular human girl except she had a perfectly proportioned body with huge, real breasts and a flawless face and a golden horn in the middle of her forehead.

"GITCH," I said, "are you seeing this too? The breasts? The horn?"

"Yes," he said, "It's a unicorn. I've heard about them in legends before. We picked the right night to come here."

We'd picked that night cuz women were giving us more problems than usual. They were either refusing to have sex with us anymore or refusing to be married to us anymore.

The unicorn completely captured my attention. I mean the horn was so golden and stuck so far out from her head flesh.

"I'm thinking about getting a lapdance with her," I told GITCH, "but maybe I need that money to make a payment on my Best Buy credit card instead. It's very past due."

"You have to get the lapdance," he said. "A unicorn may never be here again."

Then I approached the unicorn and told her I wanted to see her horn closely and privately.

"Alright, baby," she said and took me into a back room.

I sat down on a couch and she got on top of my lap and the horn was right there at eye level and it looked like it was about to poke my face.

"Can I squeeze it?" I said.

"Yes," she said.

I gripped my hand around it and it was not fragile, it was very firmly stuck in there. Then I noticed her boobs and they seemed firmly stuck on her too.

"Damn, what size are these?" I asked.

"Abnormally large for my frame," she said.

"Do all unicorns have boobs this big?"

"No, mine are this big because I just had a baby unicorn."

"Did the baby's horn poke you on the way out of your vagina?"

"Yes."

"And you feed the baby with your big boobs?"

"Yes."

Then she squeezed a boob with both hands and a white droplet came out of the nipple.

"Can I taste it?" I asked.

"Yes."

She squeezed more out on her finger and put the finger in my mouth. It was sweet.

"Can I suck on them?"

"Will you tip me extra?"

"Yeah, I like how money makes you do things you wouldn't normally do."

Then she put the nipple into my mouth and I sucked hard and milk came out. It had a great flavor and I wanted to drink as much of it as I could.

"Mmm," she said.

"Oh," I said. "Did that turn you on?"

"Yes."

"Does it turn you on when the baby sucks on it?"

"I'm embarrassed to say, but yes."

"It makes you think about sex around your baby."

"Yes. I've heard there's a science behind it. Certain chemicals are released by nipple stimulation. I can't help it. I have to masturbate right after feeding."

"I like how you're not in control of your sexual feelings."

"I know. Me too."

I had to be near those breasts long enough to remember exactly what they looked like later. I was nursing on them for as many songs as I could possibly afford. Then I had to pay her and go.

"Thanks, baby," she said.

"Thanks, Unicorn," I said.

Then I went back to GITCH and told him it was time to leave.

"What happened back there?" he asked.

"A once-in-a-lifetime experience," I said.

Then I rushed to drop him off and get back home so I could jerk off. I'd been pretty drunk so I probably only 60% remembered what the boobs looked like by then, but it was enough to cum good. Then when I calmed down I realized I'd totally forgotten she'd also had a horn. I tried to imagine that too, but couldn't at all. I know I just said it was long and golden, but I'm just imagining, it might not've been. I actually can't remember if it was black or red or fat or skinny. I can't remember if it was shaped like an ice cream cone or a bowling ball. I actually can't remember if she had a horn at all.

Me and GITCH are always having girl problems and go back to the strip club a lot, but we've never seen a Unicorn again.

"Well," GITCH said recently, "at least you remember her boobs."

"I don't even remember those anymore," I had to say.

8 / SMELLED

This weekend the cab smelled.

I got in on Friday night and it didn't take long before it started to smell like shit. Really like shit. Like poop. Like someone pooped inside the cab instead of into a toilet.

It didn't smell all the time. That would've been unbearable and I would've switched the car out for a loaner. No, it would have a normal cab smell most of the time. But it seemed to be whenever there were multiple passengers an odorous cloud would materialize and then a guy in the back would go, "Who farted?"

Everyone in the car would deny it. The smell would linger and worsen and then everyone would have to put their window down to get some air in and maybe blow out the smell. But the smell wouldn't blow out. It would just stay there right in front of everyone's noses.

"C'mon," someone would say, "who farted?"

And still no one would confess.

"It's alright," someone would say, "just confess, I won't judge, I just have to know."

And still no one would confess.

"It was Joe!" someone would say.

"No, it wasn't," Joe would say.

"Shut up, Joe. You always fart."

"It wasn't me, dude. I swear."

"Was it you?" they'd ask me.

"No," I'd say, "I always admit it when I fart."

And they'd believe me.

"Seriously," someone would say, "it smells like someone shit their pants in here. It smells like digestion and swamps. It smells like the heart of the sewers. It smells like something that's about to poison our lungs and kill all of us right now."

Then we'd get to their stop and everyone would get out of the car as fast as possible, pushing and stumbling on their way out.

"I'm sorry," the last person out would say.

"It's alright," I'd say.

"It was our friend Joe," they'd say. "He always farts."

"Okay," I'd say and then they'd pay and leave.

Then when I was alone again I'd stop to sniff everywhere, the vents and under the seats and under the hood, but strangely nothing would smell strongly anymore. There was no way to find the source of the smell. Maybe it *was* just a fart, I'd think. But soon more passengers would come in and the smell would return and the same fart-blame scenario would take place. And then I knew it was the taxi that was farting.

I didn't know how to stop it. In my five years of driving cab I knew a multitude of ways a Ford Crown Victoria can go wrong but I didn't know about this. How can a gas and oil combustion engine possibly make smells exactly like a human butt? Is this something everyone else knows?

It was so bad, but for some reason I decided not to take the car in to get shopped. I didn't even ask another driver what they thought of it. I didn't even bother to spray the air freshener. For some reason I just took it. I don't know why, but I sat there in the intermittent shit fumes and took it and took the commotion from the passengers and never admitted I knew what it was. Me and my nose just took it all night. Making 318 dollars in the smell. Going home then driving again the next two nights in the smell. And not even trying to breathe until Monday at 2:19 AM. The smell is probably going to be there on Tuesday night when I work again and I'll take it again. $54 in the smell, taking it. Busy graduation weekend, take it. Week after that, take it. Taking stink to pay Best Buy credit card late fees and interest. Stink. Whole summer, take it. I'll never know what and why the smell. Ongoing fumes and scent. I should know more and be better. Me, big failure in the smell, my shit, my nose, my shame, my coverups, my hell. I'll keep doing it and not say anything."

9 / WEEKEND AT FAIRY'S

I always go for the fairies. The little winged flying girls who live in the depths of the forest. The ones created when a god fucks a tree. Fairies are immortal and they don't have to follow the rules of being human and they can just dance and be free. Their wings kind of remind me of The Goddess of Faith's, My Guardian Angel Who Loves Me No Matter What. And they come to poetry readings a lot.

One time I did a performance and I wore a pair of wings. They were white and feathery and I'd gotten them at my favorite costume store in Boulder, The Ritz. I went up to the microphone and read something about the misery of taxi driving in a loud, confident voice and shook my shoulders so the wings would flap and make it seem like I was just about to make my big launch into the sky. There was a fairy in the audience who saw it and came up to me afterward.

"Hey," she said, "Do you wanna go back to the woods with me?"

"Alright," I said.

I left my wings on so she'd still think I was a fairy too. And then we drove up the canyon into The Mountains to her home. I had to park the car at the end of a dirt road and then we headed into the woods on foot. It was dark and full of leaves and branches and I followed her flashlightless ahead. Then we stopped at a big twisted tree. It had a face in it, knots that represented eyes and a mouth and it made the tree look suspicious of me.

"This is where I live," she said, "You like?"

"Yeah," I said, "Where's your bed?"

"The ground."

"Oh."

I'd been in similar situations with fairies before and it always made me think about television.

"Let's take off our clothes and lay down," she said.

"Alright," I said.

And then we stripped and got on her bed and the dirt and stones and pine cones dug into our skin. And her body was very well shaped and right next to me, but for some reason I was thinking about *Weekend at Bernie's,* the 80s movie about two dudes pretending like this one dead dude is really alive.

The fairy looked at me and her eyes were shiny and her dreadlocks were rainbow-colored and her handmade dress glittered in the moonlight.

"Let's compare our fairy adventures," she said.

"Alright," I said.

And then she started telling me about all the different woods she'd been in. The Rocky Mountain woods. The California redwoods. The Central Park woods. The Arizona petrified woods. And the South America rainforest woods.

"What woods have you been to?" she asked.

"I was in the no-woods of the Sahara Desert," I said.

It was the best woods card I had to play.

"Oh, cool," she said. "I was in the no-woods of the moon once."

"The moon? Like the one Neil Armstrong landed on?"

"Yes."

The moon, the barren satellite above planet Earth that requires rocket ship wings to reach. It made me keep thinking about *Weekend at Bernie's*. Bernie and his sunglasses. Bernie and his mustache. Bernie and his captain's hat.

When she snuggled up closer to me like it was time for sex, I could only shiver and cling to her attractive body just for the heat of it. I could only think about a tropical harebrained scheme to make a fortune and then we fell asleep.

The next day she woke me up at the very moment when the sun rose.

"Hey, let's chop wood," she said.

Then she pointed to an axe and the infinite amount of trees surrounding us. It made me think of the cartoon *He-Man* and how he has to wave his sword in the air and say, "By the power of Grayskull..." to make his cowardly pet Cringer turn into the ferocious Battlecat.

"I don't know," I said.

I noticed a whole pile of already chopped wood nearby.

"Looks like we already have enough, right?" I said.

"Yeah, but chopping wood is so fun and therapeutic," she said. "Swing, chop, swing, chop. The rhythm of it, the use of muscles."

It made me think of *Seinfeld*. That one episode where George decides to do the opposite of all his instincts and finally starts to find success.

"I don't really feel like it," I told the Fairy.

"Oh," she said. "Do you want to start the fire then?"

"No, not really."

Then she started the fire herself. Gathering big logs and small sticks and creating friction to make a spark and then blowing so the flames could spread. I sat in front of it and when it got going sometimes the smoke would blow in my face and make me cough.

It made me think about watching the Cleveland Cavaliers in their glory years of the late 80s/early 90s. The Mark Price, Brad Daugherty, Larry Nancy, Hot Rod Williams, Craig Ehlo teams that always won a lot of regular season games only to get beaten by Michael Jordan's Chicago Bulls in the playoffs.

"I want to have sex with you," she said.

"Great," I said.

"But before I have sex I first like to discuss our earliest sexual encounters."

"Alright."

Then she started telling me about herself at thirteen years old having lots of sex. She had the beginnings of breasts and pubic hair and older guys liked it and fucked her. They'd take her out in a car and tell her about Jack Kerouac and then fuck her. A guy and a guy and a girl would give her alcohol and ecstasy and then fuck her. A guy trained by NASA would take her to the lunar surface and fuck her. She was excited and proud about every detail.

"What about you?" she said.

"Oh, you know," I said.

"No, I don't know. Who did you fuck when you were thirteen years old?"

"Well, nobody."

"Why not?"

"I wasn't thinking about sex yet."

"What were you thinking about?"

"I guess I was just thinking about TV."

"TV? Like a television?"

"Yeah, my mom and dad and brother and I would sit in the living room on our seats. Big leather chair, rocking chair, couch. And we'd eat popcorn and drink cream sodas and watch a show that was on TV or a movie we'd rented. *Full House, The Muppet Show, Jeopardy, the Summer Olympics. The Little Mermaid, The Karate Kid, Big, Days of Thunder, Weekend at Bernie's.*"

"Oh, drag."

"It wasn't a drag actually. It was really comfortable. I mean it was really great. I mean we genuinely felt joy watching it. We felt relaxed and happy. Sometimes I really want to have that back."

"Weird."

We didn't end up having sex that day or night. We ate handfuls of nuts and bee pollen and then fell asleep.

The next day she let me sleep in late and it was probably the afternoon. She'd already chopped more wood and made a fire.

"So, do you want to like fly with me now or what?" she said.

"Fly?"

"Yes, rise into the air and start zooming thru the trees. That's my favorite thing to do."

Then to demonstrate she started flapping her wings and they lifted her off the ground.

"Actually," I said. "I don't have the ability to do that."

"You're not really a fairy are you?" she said.

"No."

And then I took my wings off and showed her they were only staying on me cuz of rubber bands around my shoulders.

"Okay," she said, "well just letting you know, I only have sex with other fairies."

"Okay," I said, "that makes sense."

Then we shrugged at each other.

"I think I'm going to go home now," I said.

She nodded and gave me an awkward hug.

Then I drove back down to my house. When I got in the door I took a deep breath and grabbed a bag of tortilla chips and went into my room. I didn't have a television anymore, but I had the Internet and looked for pictures of naked celebrities and found some and jerked off. Then I went to a site where I could illegally stream *Weekend at Bernie's* and I watched it and it made me laugh. After that I felt tired and crawled into bed. I tucked myself underneath my blankets and sheets and my warm and heavy comforter. And my back sank into a soft mattress and my head sank into a soft pillow.

"Ahh," it all made me say.

But I couldn't get to sleep. I couldn't stop thinking about how far away my family and Angel were.

"Who here is going to like me *this* way?" I couldn't stop thinking.

10 / MY FINGERNAILS ARE SCATTERED ALL OVER THE STREETS OF BOULDER, COLORADO

As I drive down the streets of Boulder I put my fingers in my mouth. I put the nail between my teeth and snip it and then tear it back until it comes off. Then I pick the nail out of my mouth and look at it. Hard and white sliver. "Mm," I say and then fling it out the car window.

Cab Stand 11th and Pearl, Fox Theatre 1135 13th, Boulder Theatre 2032 14th, University of Colorado 1700 Colorado Libby Hall Farrand Hall Baker Hall...

I've been a professional driver in this town for 10 years and that means 10 years worth of fingernails have been flung out on its streets. There could be so many still out there. Lost in the grass, stuck inside birds' nests, piling up in great drifts in the alleyways. How long does it take for a fingernail to decompose anyway? They seem a little bit indestructible, don't they?

Boulder Community Hospital 1100 Balsam, Boulder Transit Center 1400 Walnut, Table Mesa Park n Ride 5170 Table Mesa, University of Colorado 1700 Colorado Sewell Hall University Memorial Center Folsom Stadium...

My nails all over town. Interrupting your day. A nail flying thru the wind at your face. Heaps of them blowing out of hand, scratching the pavement, climbing up the walls of buildings. No one knows who they belong to, do they? No one's doing the DNA test, right?

Outback Saloon 3141 28th, Darkhorse 2922 Baseline, Harpo's 2860 Arapahoe, St. Julian Hotel 900 Walnut, Boulder Outlook Hotel 800 28th, Boulderado 2115 13th, CU 1700 Colorado Engineering Center Music building Wolf Law...

So many nails. Ten fingers and they keep growing back endlessly and now stronger from daily multi-vitamins, SCRATCH. Why not just trim them with a clipper and throw them in my bedroom trash can? No. They need to be in my mouth. There are people punching my car out there cuz I won't pick them up. There are passengers who demand small talk even when I'm in my "quiet mood." So many pizzas years ago got there late. And my novel needs to be finished now. My novel needs to be finished before now. It needs to be finished but I'm always driving a car for work instead.

29th Street Mall 1700 29th, Taco Bell 2450 Baseline, Frasca Food and Wine 1738 Pearl, Flagstaff House 1138 Flagstaff, Naropa University main campus 2130 Arapahoe, apartment 2011 Goss, house 2060 Grape, San Lazaro Trailer Park 5505 Valmont

Come here, nail! Suck suck snip. Fling. Take that, finger and body. Take that, Boulder, I'm nailing your nailtown and nailstreets with my nailnails. I confess it is me who is causing the city's Nail Issue. And I'm not going to stop because they don't stop growing... and IT doesn't stop. You know what IT is, right?

11 / CARELLI'S FIRE!

Carelli's is the Italian restaurant in the shopping center on 30th Street and Baseline, right across from the Williams Village Dorms. And there is a fiery cauldron outside its front door. Orange flames shooting up into the night until they close. I can see it in the distance as I'm driving down Baseline and it makes me think maybe I should finally go in there one of these nights. I've never actually gone in but I appreciate the fires drawing me in.

Carelli's Fire. A landmark for me. Passing it every weekend in the cab. Driven past so many times I forget it's there sometimes. How can it not be invisible when you've just picked up the freshman who says, "I bet you make mad bank at this job"? And you have to say, "No, man, I'm poor, I'm one of those poor people you hear about."

Carelli's Fire!

When you look at it that way, the words in that order, capitalized with an exclamation point, it's the Mythic Knowledge! The Hot Soul of the Gods! Something that can save me, I think!

Ohhh, The Fires of Marketing make me look and I like it.

Restaurant, you don't have to do this torch, but you do.

Carelli's Fire, a never ending supply of gas.

"Look at that," I'll say to all the college girls jammed into the backseat. "It's so bright orange. So wildly rising and falling. Where will the wind tell the flames to go next?!"

But they don't answer, cuz they're not listening. And maybe Carelli's Fire is only seen by me.

Carelli's Fire, some instinct from within that needs to be witnessed with eyes and escapes out of me as hallucination.

That's it. I'm the only one who sees it. The elements of me projected outward I'm sure.

And where will it ignite next?

Pearl Street Fire?

University of Carellirado?

Infernosfree Poetry Bookstore Weekly Tuesday Open Cauldron?

Oh man, next time I pass Carelli's I'm going to stop the cab and get out. I'm going to jump right into the flames and make sure they burn my whole body. "Carelli's Fire!" I'll yell out in pain.

Carelli's Fire, I'm going to find the hostess to get seated.

Carelli's Fire, do you have gluten-free pasta?

Carelli's Fire, show me your hot menu, I'm finally coming in.

12 / THE GIANT

"Fuck me harder!" The Giant said.

"Okay," I said and tried to lunge into her with more force.

I didn't like The Giant very much, but there I was trying to fuck her hard anyway.

"C'mon!" she said, "put more strength into it. Use more of your muscles."

"I'm trying," I said and clutched the sheets and dug in my knees to try to get more leverage.

The Giant was an enormous woman. She had an enormous head. Enormous hips. Enormous breasts. Enormous bush. Enormous will. Enormous. Enormous. Enormous.

"Choke me!" The Giant said.

"What do you mean?" I said.

"Put your whole forearm against my throat and press down. I don't want to be able to breathe anymore."

"Won't that hurt?"

"Shut up and do it!"

I didn't like causing pain to other human beings at any moment for any reason, but I did what she said.

"No, you're doing it wrong," she said. "Harder. Be more of a man. Subdue me."

She was gagging and her neck was getting red, and it was making my dick go soft but I did it anyway.

"No!" she said. "Subdue me. Like this."

Then The Giant grabbed me by my shoulders, flipped me underneath her, and started trying to choke *me* with her enormous hands. I had to fight to regain control and save my life. I had to flex my biceps and legs and guts as hard as I could to get her off me, but I wasn't strong enough. Goddammit, The Giant was so enormous. The only way to free myself was to lean my head up to her enormous hanging tits and grab a nipple by the teeth.

"Ouch!" she said and pulled my hair.

But I wouldn't let go. I bit down on the nipple until it bled. It was the only way to win. Red liquid on my mouth and her chest.

"You're going too far!" she said.

Then finally I released and she slapped my face.

"I'm sorry," I said.

"Don't be," she said. "It was just starting to get hot."

"What?"

"Yeah, now fuck me again."

We both looked down at my soft dick.

"Guess you'll just have to eat me out then," she said.

"Okay," I said and she shoved me down between her enormous thighs and I put my mouth on her enormous pussy.

"Fe Fi Fo Fum, I want you to make me cum," she said.

"Okay," I said and licked her clitoris with speed and finesse.

The Giant thrashed and moaned and was building up to a release. I started vibrating my tongue wildly and it sent her over the edge. Her enormous pelvis lifted up and she screamed, "AHHH!"

And then liquid started spraying out of her all over my face. I tried to flinch out of the way but there was just an enormous amount of it. One wave after another squirting out, soaking me and the sheets. When she was finished she made me grab a towel and sop it up.

"You did good, little boy," she said.

"Thanks," I said. "I'm glad you were able to have an orgasm."

"Oh, Fe Fi Fo Fum, you didn't make me cum. You just made me squirt. It's different. You'll have to be a lot better to make me cum."

"Okay," I said and tried to find a bigger towel to wipe up the mess.

"Now, little boy," she said, "I know you loved having sex with me just now. But let's be clear about one thing. You're not allowed to get feelings for me."

"Okay."

"You're not allowed to get all romantic and try to make me your girlfriend."

"Okay."

"You need to be a bigger man, little boy, and just enjoy sex without any other attachment."

"Okay."

"I'm glad we have this understanding, little boy. I'd like to have sex with you again sometime."

"Okay," I said and waited for The Giant to fall asleep so I could escape.

13 / MOHAWK

"Hey, get a mohawk."

"What?"

"Shave your whole head except for one strip of hair down the middle."

"Really?"

"Make it bright blue with high razor sharp spikes."

"That will look strange, tho."

"You are strange. The mohawk will look exactly like how you feel inside."

"I do like punks. They don't care if mainstream culture shames them."

"Yes, Mohawk. It's you against the world."

"Am I punk enough, tho?"

"Punks can't do jobs well and get fired. They have trouble getting people to love them. And their art is very weird. Punks aren't capable of normal success so they value abnormal success."

"Mohawk."

"Like an Indian warrior."

"Like Travis Bickle."

"Do it."

"That'll be it, tho. I won't be able to pretend I'm not an outsider anymore."

"A regular haircut hasn't done anything for you anyway."

"Like Sid Vicious"

"Mohawk yourself. Mohawk your writing. Mohawk the world"

"I am Mohawk."

"You *are* Mohawk!"

"I'm Monsterhawk!"

"You scare me!"

"Rohhrhawk!!"

"Yeah!!!"

"I won't, tho."

"I know."

"I'm still too scared to not fit in."

"I know."

"Maybe one day."

"Yes, Mohawk one day."

14 / THE FORTUNE TELLER

Years ago My College Roommate went to see The Fortune Teller. She looked into her crystal ball and it showed his past and his future. She would not tell him exactly what she saw, but she did give him a warning...

"STOP!" she said. "Stop what you're doing and start helping people right now."

My friend had gone to grad school to be a Buddhist holyman but then he started working at a company that was trying really hard to make money.

"Why should I believe you?" my friend asked The Fortune Teller.

"Because," she said. "I know you work in marketing and I know you have a twin and I know you've lost a kidney and I should not know these things."

I saw my friend right after it happened and his mouth was stuck wide open and his eyes could no longer blink.

"I have to change everything," he said.

"Wow," I said.

And then I wanted to go to The Fortune Teller too.

I found her in a dark and mysterious underground lair beneath the New Age bookstore. There she was, an ugly, old crone with long, white hair and pupil-less eyes. I was frightened and repulsed but when she summoned me forward with her bony finger I followed.

"Come sit down," she said in a frail rasp.

I sat down at her table. There was a silk-covered crystal ball between us.

"What do you want to know about your future?" she asked.

"I want to know how famous my writing is going to make me," I said.

She removed the cloth from the ball and looked deeply into it.

"Hmm," she said, "I don't see anything about that."

"Oh no, does that mean I'm going to fail?"

"I don't know. For some reason the ball is only showing me about love."

"Oh...that."

"I see all the lovers of your life, past, present, and future."

"They've been pretty awful so far, haven't they?"˄

"I see you being awful too."

"Me? But I'm an *innocent*."

"I see you trying to make them your Compliment Slaves."

"I don't even know what that is."

"You lock them in a room and only let them out to give you compliments."

"I don't do that."

"You need them to say things like, 'Jonathan, you're such a good writer,' so you feel like a good writer."

"I don't *need* them to…"

"You need them to say, 'Jonathan, you're so smart, so strong, so sexually attractive.' You must own them because you need the compliments so badly and all the time. You cannot compliment yourself."

"I…"

"Jonathan, tell me all about your day. Tell me about your hopes and worries and I'll make them mine too. Jonathan, how can I help you? What do you need? Jonathan, you're perfect."

"No."

"Jonathan, you *are* alright. I love your stuffed animals and your costumes and your iTunes playlist. Jonathan, your cock fits so well inside of me. Jonathan, Jonathan, Jonathan, I love you and only you."

"Stop it!"

"You need them to take care of you. You need them to rescue you. You need them to save you from your Beast. It is so much pressure, of course they don't want to be your girlfriend."

"You're wrong, crone!"

"I am not. I know you deliver pizzas, and I know you love the music from *The Little Mermaid* soundtrack and I know your mother's name is Every Single Second of Every Single Hour. And I should not know these things."

Then my mouth was stuck open and my eyes couldn't blink.

"Okay, I believe you," I said. "What's my future?"

"You will never be in love…" she said.

"Oh god, no!"

"Unless you summon your True Love."

"Alright, who is it?"

"You know."

"You mean I've already met her?"

"Yes, she is the one who loves you no matter what."

"The Goddess of Faith, My Guardian Angel?"

"Yes. I can see her wings in my ball."

"But she's not a human girl."

"It doesn't matter. You and The Angel share the same soul. She is the only one you can truly be in love with. And The Beast cannot appear when she is with you."

"I don't even know how to summon her. I think I've been doing it by accident so far."

"For The Angel to come it is simple. You must take care of yourself. You must be gentle with yourself. And then you must say the magic words."

And then she told me the magic words.

"That sounds hard and complicated," I said.

"It is the only way."

"But regular people don't have to become enlightened to find love. It's not fair. It's supposed to be easy. And The Angel might not even be real. I want a real flesh-and-blood hot college chick to love me."

"Fair or unfair, it has been revealed in the ball."

"But…"

"But nothing, summon her, summon her, summon her…"

The Fortune Teller just kept saying "summon her" over and over until I paid and left. And then I tried to think about all the ways she might be a fraud so I wouldn't have to listen to her.

15 / I LIKED THE BOULDER FLOOD!

I liked how there was a flood.

How it just kept raining and it was harmless at first and suddenly it was a disaster.

I liked how I was driving the cab and all of a sudden there was deep water on the roads and my wheels could barely go thru it.

I liked how my car got stuck cuz it was too deep and how I had to force the gas pedal down all the way to get it to move forward 1 mph or else it would've sunk for good and I woulda been stranded on top of the roof calling out for help.

I was terrified when I got home from work and I liked it a lot.

I like how I went on the Internet and saw pictures of other cars stuck and reports of evacuations and I liked how someone had died and how a mudslide had rammed right into his mountain home and suffocated his mouth with mud and rocks until he didn't have enough oxygen to be alive.

"Yes!" I said, "It's finally happening, the destruction of it all."

And finally I only had to worry about the water in front of me instead of money, women, and artistic success and everyone would understand.

I liked it, road closings and dams breaking and ruined basement carpets.

I liked taking pictures the next day of dead animals and how garbage cans were in the creek and crayfish were on the sidewalk and the prairie dogs all drowned.

I liked not going to work cuz it was too dangerous.

I liked putting a bucket under my leaking ceiling and letting it fill up and then dumping it in the toilet every hour or so and I liked how the drops from the ceiling would spray out a little and get my shoulder moist.

I liked the sound of helicopters bringing in evacuees to the airport.

I liked the sounds of pumps and rushing creek and more rain pounding down.

I liked the carpet and drywall piles at the end of every driveway.

I liked the police cars and back hoes, the warnings from the National Weather Service on the radio and that screech of noise that precedes them.

I liked hearing all the stories from people in the cab and how almost everyone had damage.

I liked smelling the mold on my damp carpet and going to Home Depot for anti-mold spray and I liked how I couldn't breathe at night cuz the mold got into the depth of my lungs and tried to multiply itself and my immune system tried desperately to expel it thru coughs and I didn't sleep at all.

I liked telling everyone in the cab about it and asking for their advice, "What do you know about mold?"

I liked how the ceiling one morning started to lump down and then crack and then the water started dripping more forcefully from more places and how the crack started to grow and how it started to turn at a right angle and it seemed like part of the ceiling might fall down right over my desk and I got the computer out of the way just in time before part of the ceiling actually did collapse and it made a big boom and wet insulation fell all over me and on my back and I had to wipe it off my t-shirt and I had to rescue as many important items as I could from the wet smelly mess and some papers of mine were destroyed forever.

I liked telling everyone about how I too was victimized and I liked getting my parents' advice and liked going to stay indefinitely at my friends' house in Broomfield.

I liked being fifteen miles away from my home and spending slightly more money on gas.

And I liked going to State Farm Insurance and I liked discussing possibly getting FEMA aid.

I liked how other people have it worse like some people lost their whole house and some people lost their whole entire lives.

I really really liked how, finally, we got to stop the big imaginary game and concern ourselves with something real like the water that was directly in front of us.

And I don't like that it's not flooding anymore and I'm mad how the sun came back out and dried everything.

I don't like how time keeps moving forward and the flood is already becoming past.

I don't like how one day soon I'll be back in the old routine and I won't even remember the flood anymore.

I don't like how I'm just gonna sit there thinking at my desk about all the things I'm supposed to be doing and how if I was someone a little more superior to myself I could be doing them: money, love, success. You know, the imaginary life, not the real life, not like the flood life.

I loved the flood, I wish it was always flood.

16 / THE SORCERESS

She came up to me after the reading in her black and purple cloak and put her hand on my arm.

"Holy shit," she said. "You're a good poet."

"Thanks," I said.

She was right. I was a good poet. People were starting to tell me that all the time. Especially young, hot girls. But none of them were becoming my girlfriend and I was skeptical about what telling me I'm a good poet really meant.

"It's like your throat chakra and heart chakra are in perfect harmony," she said.

"Ha!" I said.

"No, seriously. There's something about you. I could tell from the first line. It makes me want to touch you."

Her hand was still on my arm the whole time. It rubbed a little.

"Who are you?" I said. "What do you want from me?"

"I'm The Sorceress and I just think you're cool."

"Sorceress? Like a manipulator of the world via magic?"

"Uh huh."

"Yeah, sure you are."

"I really am a real sorceress. I make potions and cast spells. When I point my wand at something it changes."

Then she took out a little twig and pointed it at a crispy brown dead leaf that had blown into the open mic. She whispered something and then the leaf suddenly turned moist and green.

"Well, that's something," I said.

Then she put her whole arm around my back and she was close and I could smell her hair and it smelled like powers.

"Here's my business card," she said.

It had her contact information and said:

THE SORCERESS

Potions and Spells

To Make the World Better

"Cool," I said and put it in my jean jacket pocket.

"Hey, have some of this," she said and handed me her drink.

"Alright, thanks," I said and took a sip.

It was chocolaty and alcoholic and I liked it and we traded sips until it was finished. Then we looked at each other. Her green eyes started to seem very meaningful and I smiled at her and she smiled back.

"Hmm," I thought. "Something feels *different* about this one."

17 / THE BEAUTY OF AUTUMN

Sometimes The Beauty of Autumn accidentally gets inside my cab. I'll pick up a passenger and a little bit of it will come in with them. There will be a drunken idiot and they'll bring in their vodka and pot stink and their slurred dick jokes and their shouting out the windows at pretty girls and police officers and their beer bottle they're about to spill on the floor. But they'll also bring in sweet apple cider and falling colorful leaves.

"I wanna fuck something that moves!" they'll say.

And I'll be like, "Wait a second…what's that next to you? A little extra crispness in the air?"

"Yeah," they'll say, "it's getting kinda chilly out there, I'm glad I brought my jacket tonight."

"The Beauty of Autumn," we'll both sigh and then relax.

I mean the cab is usually the opposite of The Beauty of Autumn. It's usually the Ugliness of All-The-Time. But sometimes this time of year even the guy who can barely walk to the car, can barely open the car's door, can barely sit upright in the backseat and says "uh, can you take me to Colorado Springs for fourteen bucks?" Even that guy brings in a little pumpkins and touchdowns with him. You have to kick his ass out but you can keep his jack o' lantern.

The Beauty of Autumn, too big and powerful to not just emerge sometimes. I don't see it most of the time cuz what does it have to do with my money and my crushes and the collective success of my local poetry scene? I need to focus on what's inside my own head in order to accomplish things. But The Beauty of Autumn is always there and pops up for five minutes when my guard is down. Driving down the highway 36 hill into Boulder, and surprise!… There's a little bit of fog hovering over the Flatirons and a ray of sunshine poking thru right down on a grove of big yellow leafed trees in an open space ranch, ahh. I think The Beauty of Autumn is trying to make me feel like I'm a finally A Part of Nature. I think it's trying to make me cry. I don't have to do anything to *make* The Beauty of Autumn happen, it's just there on its own ready for my tears.

It makes me want to survive on nothing but The Beauty of Autumn. Halloween. The new school year. Indian Summer. Foliage. Flannel shirt. Virgo, Libra, Scorpio. My high school friend Chris once said, "Fall is the best time to be in love." Gently moving toward the acceptance of Death-Winter. The leaves fly at your head and you duck out of the way, rakes! Caramel apple. Hay ride.

And I realize how far from this I usually am. I never write about the beauty of a season and might not ever again. Maybe one day when I'm really old and don't care about machines and winning and the smell of shit anymore.

The Beauty of Autumn. Here it is now. Snuck inside this poetry book a little bit today. Let's all feel it for just a second…

There.

18 / WAND

"Here," The Sorceress said and handed me a little wooden twig, "you can have this wand."

I looked at it. It was bare of bark and had many forks. It looked like a little lightning bolt.

"It's my old one," she said. "It's sort of broken."

I noticed the end had snapped a little but was still kinda dangling on there.

"Does it still work?" I asked.

"Yes," she smiled, "there's still a little magic left in it."

"Cool, thank you."

Then I put it in my jean jacket's inside pocket that also had her business card and a poem she'd written about making the world better. That pocket had always been the "snack pocket," cuz I'd put a couple of gluten-free granola bars in there when I'd go to work. But now it was becoming the "magic pocket." And maybe a dove would fly out of it eventually.

The next day at home I took out the wand and looked at it again and waved it around. Then I thought I'd try some spells.

I pointed the wand straight ahead and concentrated hard.

"Her heart is healed. Her heart is open. Her heart is ready for me."

Then I pointed it at myself.

"My heart is healed. My heart is open. My heart is ready for her."

Then I pointed it up at the ceiling.

"Everyone's hearts are healed. Everyone's hearts are open. Everyone's hearts are ready for everyone."

Then I danced around and waved the wand wildly in all directions.

"I am a powerful wizard now and this is The Truth!"

When I felt like I'd unleashed enough magic I put the wand back in my pocket. Then I grabbed a granola bar and left the house and I couldn't wait to see if the spell had worked.

19 / THINGS THAT GET LEFT IN THE BACK OF MY CAB

A lot of things get left in the back of my cab. Phones. Money. The iPod I currently use. Sunglasses. Umbrellas. Lighters. Earrings. One time someone left behind a totem pole.

A really fucked-up drunk guy I picked up at the cab stand brought it in with him. He tried to tell me what it meant.

"Some people are eagles on top of the totem pole and some people are slugs on the bottom," he said. "What are you?"

"I'm a human," I said. "I'm not on a totem pole."

"Oh, you're something on the totem pole. Everyone is."

"Bullshit," I said.

Then I dropped the guy off at a mysterious corner on the outskirts of town and went back to pickup someone else from the cab stand.

"Hey," the next passenger said, "there's a totem pole back here."

"Shit," I said, "the last guy forgot his goddamn totem pole. Just try to push it aside or something."

"Okay, but it's big."

"I know."

The guy pushed it aside I guess but he mentioned it again when I dropped him off.

"That thing is scary," he said. "The bird on it was looking at me."

"I'm sorry," I said.

Then I went into the backseat and got a good look at it. On top was the Eagle with its wings spread wide and its beak ready to attack. The guy was right, the eyes looked right at you and made you shiver. The only thing I could think to do was to put it in the trunk. It was made of really heavy wood and it was hard to lift. And it was too big for the trunk to be able to close and you could hear it rattling around back there as I drove. Passengers would ask about it and I had to say "totem pole."

I wouldn't be able to take it to the lost and found until the next day and had to take the totem pole home with me. I transferred it from the cab to my car. It hurt my back. It put a splinter in my finger.

"You disgusting thing," I said to it.

But the next day I went out to the car and saw the totem pole sticking out of my trunk in the daylight.

Eagle,

then Bear,

then Wolf,

then Crow,

then Fox,

then Beaver,

then Fish,

then Frog,

then Slug.

There was such an order to it. It had such certainty. And it was so skillfully carved.

"Hmm," I thought, "maybe I want to keep this for myself now."

I took it inside and put it in the corner of my bedroom and the totem pole went all the way to the ceiling. Then I started looking at it every day. I wondered which of the animals was me. Sometimes I was Eagle and sometimes I was Slug. I was never anything in between. I wanted to be Eagle all the time tho. I felt bad that taxi driving wasn't an Eagle kinda job and I didn't have Eagle money. I felt bad I didn't have a SHEagle in my life. I actually felt like a Slug most of the time.

I wanted to be around the totem pole all the time. Maybe, I thought, if I studied it enough I would understand how to become Eagle. So I put it on my back and brought it with me to work.

"Nice pole," passengers would say.

"Thanks. Some people are eagles and some people are slugs," I'd tell them.

"I know," they'd say.

And some of them had their own totem pole wisdom to add.

"You gotta be Slug before you can be Eagle."

"You've gotta be born Eagle."

"Eagle is full of shit. Eagle just hunts small helpless animals. You actually want to be more in the Crow-Bear range."

"Never ever give up your dream to be Eagle. No one steps on Eagle's head."

Every night bringing it in the cab and then putting it back in the bedroom so it could watch over me as I slept. But some nights I would wake up and see the totem pole and all the animals staring at me and I'd think something isn't right about this. I'd think about how it was just made out of wood. Even the Eagle. And there are real Eagles of flesh and feathers soaring thru the wilderness of Alaska.

Then one night I randomly gave a ride to the original totem pole guy again.

"Oh," he said, "I see you have my old totem. Do you like it? Are you in love with it?"

"No," I said, "I hate it. It just makes me feel bad about myself. Thank god you're here to take it back."

"I don't want it back. That thing is cursed. I've felt so good about myself since I lost it."

"Well, I don't want it either."

"Maybe drop it off in another cab?"

"I don't want another cab driver to get it and feel bad about themselves."

"Maybe we should destroy it then?"

"I think we should."

Then me and the guy went to his place and grabbed some axes and took the totem into a field and started chopping. I took care of those big eagle wings first thing and then drove the blade into the other animals faces 'til they were just sawdust. It was hard work and me and the guy were breathing heavy afterward.

"What do you think?" I said. "Is it destroyed?"

"I think so," he said.

Then we shook hands and went our separate ways. And I immediately felt so much lighter. I felt like I could fly.

But it didn't take long before another drunk fucker brought his own totem pole in the cab again.

"The Hawk is on top," he said. "And the Worm is on the bottom."

"Don't you dare leave that thing in the back of my cab," I said.

20 / THE SORCERESS'S KISS

Me and The Sorceress were sitting in my car in a parking lot. She looked into my back seat.

"Wow," she said. "Look at all the stuff you have back there."

"Yeah," I said. "Most of it's stuff that got left in the cab and I just took it."

"Someone left all these cell phones?"

"Yeah."

"Someone left this fedora?"

"Uh huh."

"Someone left this giant wooden eagle wing?"

"There's a long story to that one."

"Someone left these soft fuzzy angel wings?"

"No, I bought those."

"Why?"

"I was trying to summon The Angel by looking like her."

As we both looked back at the angel wings the sides of our heads touched. Her hand was feeling the soft feathers and I put my hand on top of it. Then she turned her hand over and grasped mine.

"Just letting you know I'm *not* going to kiss you tonight," I said.

"Good," she said. "Cuz I was going to resist if you tried."

"We're not going to kiss, but if one or the other of us at any point feels like kissing I think we should say it out loud. Just say 'I want to kiss you' and then the tension can be released and we can continue just hanging out in this parked car."

"Alright, good plan."

"Let's try saying it once just for practice."

"No, cuz then you're going to kiss me."

"No, I won't," I said but she didn't say it.

Then we went back to front seat and I started kissing her neck.

"Hey," she said. "You're kissing me."

"No," I said. "This doesn't count. When I said 'kiss' I only meant on the mouth."

"Oh, okay."

Then I kissed her everywhere except her mouth and she let me. Then I put my lips right on top of her lips but I didn't pucker or push forward.

"That's so close to a kiss," she said.

"But it's not," I said.

Her lips were shaking underneath mine.

"I really want to kiss you, tho," I said.

"I really want to kiss you too," she said.

"Alright, but you know we can't."

"I know."

Then I took my hand and went feeling around her legs. I found a secret chute in her cloak that accidentally led all the way to her vagina. It was very wet and she let me start rubbing it. And she kept moaning and saying "thank you."

And right when she was on the verge of something I leaned in and pressed my lips firmly against hers.

"But we're not supposed to..." she said.

"Oh," I said and pulled away.

"No, don't stop. I want you to."

"Alright."

And then we kissed all the way. Mouths open, tongues inside rubbing each other in synch. While my finger vibrated on her clitoris and made her body spasm.

"Ahh!" she went, "THANK YOU!"

"You're welcome," I said into her mouth.

And then we both pulled apart.

"I kissed you," I said.

"I know," she said.

"I broke you down."

"Or did I break you down?"

"No, I broke you down."

21 / THE GAS STATION GUY WATCHES ME PLAY THE LOTTERY

There's a 24-hour gas station next to cab headquarters and every day I top off the tank there before parking the car for the night. The same guy always works the early morning shifts. The old guy with the mustache and the accent. I've paid him for gas hundreds of times but I never knew his name.

"How are you, my friend?" he'll say.

"Okay," I'll say. "You?"

"Okay," he'll say.

Then we won't say anything more. He'll have large bags under his eyes and he'll slouch. Often he'll just be sitting in a chair and staring at nothing. His eyes will look yellow and sick. I'll wonder if he's as exhausted as I am.

One night I was gassing up and had an urge. I hadn't made enough money that night. I'd made enough to survive another day but I wanted more. I wanted to be able to afford to go to a restaurant every night of the week. I wanted to finally pay off the entire balance of my Best Buy credit card. I wanted to live in a house just like the one we all used to live in with my Doctor Dad. And I really wanted enough money to pay a competitive salary to everyone in The Boulder Poetry Scene. And I could only think of one route by which to possibly achieve this.

"Hey man," I said to The Gas Station Guy, "I'm gonna get a lottery ticket tonight."

His eyes suddenly opened up and looked at me

"Which kind?" he asked.

"This one," I said and pointed. "The twenty dollar scratch off."

I gave him twenty dollars and then he handed me the ticket.

"Good luck, my friend," he said.

"The most I've ever won on one of these is a hundred dollars," I said. "It was the best day of that month."

The Gas Station Guy nodded.

"I kinda really want to win the full one million dollar top prize, tho," I said.

"This will be a winner," he said. "I know it."

I looked into his eyes and they were now clear and white and had total certainty. I dug out my keys. I was ready to begin.

First you had to scratch the winning numbers and then you had to scratch the other numbers and if they matched you got the prize shown below the number. You might also scratch and it's not a number but an instant win symbol.

My key scraped over the surface of the ticket and the silver dust flew up. The Gas Station Guy leaned over the counter and watched closely. I went thru the first row of numbers, but none of them matched.

"C'mon," The Gas Station Guy pumped his fist.

I continued scratching the next row, but still nothing matched. Every number was one off. It didn't have *the feel* of a winner.

"You can still get instant win," The Gas Station Guy said.

I scratched the next row and still there was no match or instant win. The Gas Station Guy banged his fist against the counter.

"Dammit," he said, "You need this."

"I know," I said.

"We work late at night for these assholes for nothing. We do not see the sun in the winter. We are so tired."

"I know!"

"Take their money. Win. We deserve it. Not them. Break even okay too. Just don't give this goddam gas station any more of your money!"

Last row: 19. 28. 4. 47. 14.

The numbers were all wrong. None of them matched. Even tho I tried as hard as I could.

The Gas Station Guy leaned back behind the counter and frowned.

"Better luck next time," he said.

"Yeah," I said.

I stuffed the ticket in my pocket so I could enter it in the extremely low odds second-chance drawing and then I went to the bathroom to take a piss. When I came back out I saw The Gas Station Guy sitting in a chair and staring at nothing again.

"Hey," I said.

"Something else?" he said.

"Jonny," I pointed at myself.

He looked over and nodded.

"Buddy," he pointed at himself.

Then I nodded.

Then he went back to staring and I went out to park the taxi for the night and go home.

22 / SEX WITH THE SORCERESS

One night after the open mic I went back with The Sorceress to her place. We went straight to her bed and started kissing and then she got out a little treasure box full of condoms.

"Put this on," she said and handed me a condom.

"Alright," I said and put my dick inside it and then put my dick inside her.

"Thank you!" she said and we started having sex.

"What turns you on?" she said as I thrusted.

"Movies about True Love," I said.

"What do you mean? Like Disney movies?"

"Yeah, like *The Little Mermaid*."

"I love that one too. But what do you like in bed?"

"I like being in True Love in bed. I don't like choking her or cumming on her face. I don't like spanking or ropes or dirty talk or anal or orgies or lingerie or anyone ordering anyone around. I just like to kiss and be inside you and feel like I'm falling head-over-heels in love."

"Aww."

And then she kissed me a lot and held me tight and it made me so hard and I had so much energy to pound away at her. We did it in every position and each time we shifted we made sure that my penis didn't leave her vagina and she thanked me the whole time. Finally she got on top of me and made sure that I was hitting just the right place inside her to give her a very loud and fulfilling orgasm. Then I pulled out and ripped the condom off and ejaculated all over her chest.

"Yes!" I said.

"That was so nice," she said and gave me a good tight hug. "I like you a lot."

"I like you too," I said.

Then we got out of the bed.

"I'm going to get some water," she said. "Do you need anything? A snack maybe?"

"Do you have any fruit?"

"Yes."

Then we went naked out to the kitchen and I noticed her butt and boobs looked very nice as she walked. She poured us both a big cup of water and then handed me an apple. Red Delicious.

"Ooh," I said.

And then I bit right into its side and it went "crack!" and it was so apple. It was so crisp and sweet and it did not let me down. I took another bite and handed it back to her and then she took a bite.

"Mm," she said and handed it back to me.

"Mm," I said. "I love apples."

"You can finish it all if you want."

"Really? Thank you."

I ate the rest of it and enjoyed every bite. She gave me a napkin to wipe off the apple's juice and then we crawled back in her bed and discussed the history of our love lives. The hopes and monsters on both sides. And she listened well and seemed to understand.

"This is going really well, isn't it?" I said.

"Yes, it is," she smiled.

And then we fell asleep holding each other.

23 / THE LEXUS BOW

Every year at Christmastime they start showing the Lexus commercials. They say something like "GIVE SOMEONE A LEXUS FOR CHRISTMAS," and show a brand new car with a huge red bow on it and someone's loved one coming out and seeing it in the driveway and going "Good Christmas present."

Me and My Roommate would be at The Trailer watching TV and the commercial would come on and one of us would say, "Are you going to get me a new Lexus this year?"

"Yeah," the other would say.

"Good, don't forget to put the giant bow on it."

"Don't worry, giant bow, got it."

"Good."

He was a delivery driver and I was a cab driver and we'd both done the other's job before too. And My Roommate barely worked at all cuz of health and laziness and it would take him an entire decade to pay for a new Lexus even if he didn't spend his money on anything else.

Every time the commercial came on it got a laugh from us. I mean our sink was leaking and the kitchen's electrical outlets didn't work.

My Roommate's 30-year-old Toyota had a hole in the bottom like the Flintstones' car and credit card companies would garnish his wages if he tried putting a penny in his checking account. There were mysterious "soft spots" all over the floor and the front step was gone and the toilet was broken. It couldn't flush anymore. But we were pooping in it anyway. There was a large pile of brown shit in there that couldn't get sucked away and it smelled. The Lexus Bow? Maybe we could've put a bow on a heap of feces but certainly not a luxury vehicle.

Hahaha, the laughs that keep a couple of poor guys going.

This was the year I finally moved out. One too many things fell apart around me—The Ceiling—and I had to escape. I think it made My Roommate really sad when I told him The Trailer Era was over and I wasn't coming back. I was his big ally in poverty, after all. And the day after I U-Hauled my last stuff out he had a severe infection that put in him in the ICU for two weeks. I tried not to think that I caused it by abandonment. I mean My Roommate was always almost dying anyway. At least three near-deaths and one of them I had to save his life by carrying his fat heavy body into my car to take him to the ER. None of the near deaths ever lead to an I've-got-to-change-everything-now epiphany, tho.

After he got out of the hospital he called me up and said I had some mail to pick up. When I got there it was one letter that was clearly a bullshit credit card offer. He told me all about his new problems and the new drugs he had to take and the new machine he'd be hooked up to for a while.

"Well, I gotta get going," I said. "I should probably get to work."

"Wait," he said and turned on the TV. "You know what time of year it is? That Lexus Bow has gotta be on here somewhere."

Then he started flipping thru all the channels looking for one that was playing the commercial. He found a Chevy Christmas commercial with snowflakes and jingle bells but there was no bow on the car.

"Well, you remember the fucking thing," he said.

"Yeah," I said.

"What color bow you want on your new Lexus this year?"

"Red," I said.

Then we both cracked up as we saw the commercial in our minds.

"Who expects us to afford this?" My Roommate shook his head.

"The Lexus People," I said.

"Yeah, fuck Them," he said.

We laughed again and felt like strong allies once again briefly.

24 / VOUCHER BOOKMARKS

I'll be reading a book in the cab and someone will come up to the window and say, "Are you free?" And I'll be like, "Yeah," and then I'll have to close the book so I can use my hands to steer the car for them. To remember where I left off I have to put some piece of paper in between the last pages I just read. And the nearest piece of paper is always a cab voucher, a mass printed slip needed for the taxi driving bureaucracy. Government and business programs that pay for people's rides. There's the yellow for sick people. The purple for old and handicapped people. And the white for miscellaneous people. I pick up a big stack of the vouchers at headquarters and almost never use them cuz nightdriving is mostly drunks who pay with their own money. The vouchers are all just sitting there in my binder waiting to be used for something. Who needs an officially manufactured bookmark from Barnes & Noble when I have these right here?

Books are an odd thing to have in a cab. What do written words have to do with accelerating and steering and braking a vehicle? What do they have to do with humbling yourself to follow directions for a route a passenger insists on but you know is wrong? What do they have to do with the roads on The Hill they never clear after a snowstorm? If I was trying to concentrate on a page of written words while driving I would crash!

I read them on my downtime and put them between the two front seats and people notice them.

"Oh, is that your homework?" they always ask.

"Overrated," they'll sometimes say.

"Oh, is that inspiration for your literary dream?" they never ask.

Sometimes I wonder if the taxi vouchers do something to the book I'm reading.

Printed Name

Signed Name

Address

Account Number

Mileage

Fare on Meter

Tip/Extras

Total Fare

Driver ID

Cab Number

Printed Name

Signed Name

Address

Account Number

Mileage

Fare on Meter

Tip/Extras

Total Fare

Driver ID

Cab Number

Are the blank boxes getting absorbed into the book? Am I accidentally reading the taxi-novel every single time? Am I helplessly receiving professional transportation tainted biographies? Are the books getting permanently marked by Making a Living?

Or maybe… The books are marking the vouchers and the paperwork is being transformed. Put one of those carbon copy credit card receipts in there for a couple weeks and my job suddenly comes out Pulitzer Prize. Yes, I have to remember *the books* are the powerful things. The book does the alchemy and turns bullshit to gold.

OH, I LIKE THIS!

I'm the Mark Twain driver. And this is the history of punk rock taxi. And I work for Yellow My Local Poet Allies' chapbooks.

This is why I write. I want to magically influence total drags. Put your tractor or beer tap or copy machine between the pages of this MeToo stories book and watch them change. The light and the dark must mix. The things of life need to blend into each other and create new things. This is serious, and I can help. Let me lend my hand.

25 / MY EYES

I was at the DMV getting my driver's license renewed and the DMV guy asked me all the usual questions...

"Height?"

"Five-six."

"Weight?"

"Like one-forty-five-ish."

"Hair?"

"Brown."

But then he got to eyes...

"Brown."

"You sure?"

"Yes."

"Cuz they look kinduv a little blue to me."

"They're not. They're brown."

"Okay," he said, " if you say so," and put the information in the computer so it could be the truth of my ID for the next five years.

I thought the guy was just color-stupid and I didn't think about my eyes again until I slept with The Sorceress. No one looks at your eyes more closely than someone you've just had sex with.

"You have green eyes," I said lying next to her on her bed.

"Yes, I do," she said. "And let me see…your eyes are…blue?"

"What? No. They're brown."

She scootched in close to get a better look.

"They're definitely not brown," she said. "They're not pure blue either. But there's a lot of blue in them."

"But they've always been all brown and eyes can't change color after you're born."

"Maybe they've always been blue."

"I've seen them in the mirror all my life tho."

"Maybe they can change."

"That would be weird."

But the next time I was in front of a mirror I looked at my eyes closely and noticed there was definitely something blue going on in there now. There were some tough old brown swirls but blue specks were everywhere trying hard to fight thru. And at a certain angle the brown disappeared altogether and my eyes were like the clear sky.

Blue.

My mom has blue eyes.

And long ago The Gods told me thru the flying creatures of the Utah Canyonlands that I was known to them as The Bluebird. Would it make sense that the more I'm in touch with my True Soul Self the more my Gods' Identity becomes evident in my physical appearance? Starting with the eyes and heading toward full-blown feather wings?

I'd had such a good fall season. Ever since The Flood I'd been doing well at life. I'd finally moved out of The Trailer. I'd started Boulder Poetry Tribe, a blog designed to make Boulder Poetry Scene feel good about itself thru journalism articles. I'd been taking my vitamins and writing well and seeing the good in life and reaching out to more people and maybe I was uplifting them. And I had this girl who really liked me.

Yes. Blue eyes finally. Deservedly.

Not that if yours aren't, it's bad, but Blue means something to me. And if eye color can change what else can?

The new eyes made me start walking into places assuming all my dreams would come true. I'd go into a bar or poetry reading or cab and look someone closely in the eyes so they could see my blue-ness and I'd say something like "Your dreams are gonna come true too. You're gonna become your color. I've seen the future and you will be your true purple or maroon or silver one day!"

"Look again at these beautiful eyes of mine!" I said the next time I saw The Sorceress. "Don't you want to just get hypnotized by them? Don't you just want to hold them or suck on them or something? Go ahead, don't you want to be My Blue Eyes' girlfriend?"

"I've been meaning to tell you," she said. "I'm not going to be your girlfriend."

"What?"

"I do like your eyes, but I just don't want to be anyone's girlfriend."

"Why not?"

"I don't want to be *had* by anyone. When you're someone's girlfriend they feel like they own you and they need you to make them happy. It's like you're their slave."

"But *I* don't do that."

"I was married for years to The Sorcerer and we just got divorced. I know how these things work. Now I've decided a Sorceress needs to focus only on her magic. She should be romantic partners with the whole earth."

"This isn't supposed to happen anymore. My heart is healed, my heart is open, and my heart is ready for you."

"I'm sorry."

"Do you see The Beast or something?"

"Who?"

"That Beast right next to me who hates me. You see him and it disgusts you, doesn't it?"

"I don't know what you mean."

"Yes, you do."

"I really don't."

"I didn't even want you at first! You must've put a spell on me."

"I didn't mean to."

"Horrible Sorcery. Dark Magic. Tricks! Don't do that to people unless you're going to love them!"

"I'm sorry."

"Just leave me alone!"

Then I had to get out of her bed and go home. I wondered if the blue eyes couldn't overcome The Curse with Girls then what possibly could? It made me look in the mirror again and see how my eyes were now full of blue specks suffocating under swirls of diarrhea-shit-poop brown. I guess they were probably always this way, I thought.

It made me want to put on a pair of sunglasses. It made me want to move back into The Trailer and turn all the lights off and put a blanket over my head too. I wouldn't be able to write anymore cuz I wouldn't be able to see a notebook or computer screen. I'd only be able to see DARK. And if anyone came to find me I'd shout at them "I'm invisible!"

I mean that was the way I always did it when something like this happened.

26 / IT'S ALRIGHT

He was having trouble breathing and they took him to the hospital.

His lungs and body were filling up with fluids and the doctors fought to keep up with it.

They found out it was cancer, started in the kidneys and spread rapidly.

For a couple months they tried things to keep him alive. Machines. Medicine. Prayers.

Someone from the family was with him at all times.

He tried to kickstart his meditation practice again.

But the cancer was really powerful and beat everything.

He died the day after they took him to hospice care.

They took his body to a funeral home and put makeup on him and put him in a suit.

And one Saturday everyone could come and see it.

And it was in New Jersey and people came from all over the country. Like from Colorado in a rental car. And it was a three-day trip and it cost money they didn't have but they did it anyway cuz he was once an important part of their lives.

And there were flowers everywhere. And there were lots of photographs.

And there were old friends and co-workers. There were family members and a wife who'd been his wife for ten months. And they were crying very hard.

And everyone got to go up to the casket and look at the body.

His curly black hair was trimmed.

His beard was shaved.

His thick framed glasses were off.

His eyes were closed.

His nose looked like plastic.

His lips looked like wax.

His mouth was shut.

The whole corpse was thirty-three years old just like me.

And it made me remember the time we both saw The Fortune Teller. And how he was supposed to quit his job and start helping people. But for whatever reason he didn't and instead advanced really far at his job. He'd had a lot of money and a big house and a beautiful wife and they got to travel all over the world on business trips. But you had to wonder if the stress of it all had killed him somehow. The stress of not doing what you're supposed to be doing. I wondered if The Fortune Teller had seen this funeral in her crystal ball.

I'd forgotten all about her until then. But then I could hear what she said so clearly again. "Compliment Slaves." "Angel." "Take care of yourself."

I went to the bathroom of the funeral home and took a long shit. Then I looked into the mirror and saw my face. I saw the lines and paleness from years of hating myself. The one and only self I get to have before I die. And it made me cry. And it made me remember the magic words.

"It's alright, Jonathan," I said to the mirror.

And then suddenly The Goddess of Faith, My Guardian Angel Who Loves Me No Matter What appeared in the bathroom with me.

"Bluebird!" she said. "It *is* alright, baby!"

And then she hugged and kissed me and my body filled with It's Alright, Baby! and it made me start to feel alright.

"Faith," I said. "I don't know where to begin. My College Roommate is dead and I've wasted so much time worrying about money, women, and art."

"It's alright. It's so alright, baby," she said and held me.

"This Sorceress broke my heart and I think I'm getting sick again."

"But it's really alright, baby."

"But I thought my eyes had turned blue and this wasn't going to happen anymore."

"Your eyes *have* changed tho. They're so blue and beautiful now."

"Are you sure?"

"Yes, I'm telling you as a Goddess who has certain knowledge of The Universe that your eyes are now blue. As blue as precious sapphire, blue as a chlorine swimming pool, blue as the Kansas City Royals' uniform, and blue as the feathers of the mountain bluebird. And they are not changing back."

Then I looked at them in the mirror again and she was right. The blue specks and the brown swirls and now my green tears were all working in harmony like two pretty little planet earths, so round and holding all of life.

"Man, I'm glad I summoned you, Angel," I said. "I'm feeling good again."

"I am always here for you," she said. "I am your True Love and that means I love you no matter what."

"Thank you," I said. "I love you so much."

And then we hugged and kissed for a very long time.

27 / ANGEL AND MERMAID

"Is this the mermaid?" The Goddess of Faith said.

"Yes," I said.

We were at The Aquarium together and looking at everything at a leisurely pace and I showed her my favorite part.

"What happens when I push the button?" she asked.

"I don't know," I said. "I think she's supposed to sing. But it didn't work before."

Then she pushed the button and nothing happened.

"It's alright, baby," she said. "Why don't *you* sing to her?"

"Me?" I looked around at all the other Aquarium People. "I don't think I'm supposed to here. I don't want to stand out."

"So? Do it anyway. I'll protect you."

"Alright, I guess so. What should I sing?"

"Sing 'The Mermaid Alive Song.'"

"Oh yeah."

And then I started singing it. And of course The Aquarium People started looking at me funny. And some laughed nervously and some got uncomfortable and walked away. But the mermaid looked right up at us and pressed her ear against the glass to listen. I kept singing and it was making her smile. And it encouraged me to sing more strongly. Then the mermaid opened her mouth and it looked like she was trying to sing along with me. And suddenly loud static started coming from a speaker next to the glass cage. And the static started to clear up and you could actually hear the mermaid's voice. And it was pitch perfect and beautiful and harmonizing with mine.

I looked back and now a crowd of Aquarium People had gathered around and they started singing too.

Mermaid alive! Mermaid alive! Mermaid alive!

"Is this really happening?" I asked The Goddess of Faith.

"Yes," she said.

"The singing and The Aquarium People are real?"

"Yes."

"The mermaid is real?"

"Yes."

"And you're real too?"

"Of course."

"Really? Cuz sometimes it doesn't seem like a woman with fish legs or an Angel with wings and halo and harp should be able to exist outside my imagination."

"Bluebird, I am the most real thing you've ever experienced."

"Alright, I believe you," I said.

And then I kept singing.

ACKNOWLEDGEMENTS

Mom & Dad

Nathaniel & Jessica & Sebastian & Xavier

All the girls who wanted to sleep with me

All the girls who refused to sleep with me

Amy Katz

Asalott

The Best Buy credit card I bought my laptop with

The Boulder Poetry Scene

Get in the Car, Helen

The Goddess of Faith, My Guardian Angel Who Loves Me
No Matter What

Kona Morris

Laurie Griffin

Marcus Palmer & Love Shovel

Mark & Sue Bernheim

Nancy Stohlman

Semicolon Magazine (who published "Things That Get Left
in the Back of my Cab")

That one pizza delivery company I used to work for

ALSO FROM LIVING DREAMS PRESS

The Lizard Thieves: Love Poems
by Amy Beth Katz

Quoth the Ravens, Goblins, and Lusty Maidens:
Best Loved Narrative Poetry
Edited by Amy Beth Katz

Voyager Tarot Companion:
Magical Verses for a Magnificent Voyage
by Lloyd R. Hegland

You are Psychic: The Art of Clairvoyant Reading & Healing
by Debra Lynne Katz

Extraordinary Psychic: Proven Techniques to
Master Your Natural Psychic Abilities
by Debra Lynne Katz

Living Dreams Press
www.livingdreamspress.com